pleasure
prolonged

Also by Cathryn Fox

PLEASURE CONTROL
PLEASURE EXCHANGE

pleasure prolonged

C A T H R Y N   F O X

red

A V O N

An Imprint of HarperCollins*Publishers*

PLEASURE PROLONGED. Copyright © 2007 by Cathryn Fox. All rights reserved. Printed in the United States of America. No part of this book may be used or reproduced in any manner whatsoever without written permission except in the case of brief quotations embodied in critical articles and reviews. For information address HarperCollins Publishers, 10 East 53rd Street, New York, NY 10022.

HarperCollins books may be purchased for educational, business, or sales promotional use. For information please write: Special Markets Department, HarperCollins Publishers, 10 East 53rd Street, New York, NY 10022.

FIRST AVON RED EDITION PUBLISHED 2007, REISSUED 2013.

Interior text designed by Diahann Sturge

The Library of Congress has cataloged the original paperback edition as follows:

Fox, Cathryn.
  Pleasure prolonged / by Cathryn Fox. — 1st ed.
    p. cm.
ISBN: 978-0-06-089855-7
ISBN-10: 0-06-089855-0

I. Title.

PR9199.4.F69P57 2007
823'.92—dc22   2006013732

ISBN 978-0-06-226560-9

13 14 15 16 17 OV/RRD 10 9 8 7 6 5 4 3 2 1

I would like to dedicate this book to you, all my readers. Without you, I wouldn't be doing what I love most, writing sexy books. I'd probably be stuck in an accounting job where I'd be grumpy every day, as opposed to only once a week. ☺

I'd only be dreaming of pursuing a writing career instead of living it, and I certainly wouldn't be able to go to the office every day in my pajamas!

Thank you all for making my dreams come true.

Cathryn

Chapter 1

A gorgeous hunk of a guy like that could make any woman forget her morals.

Erin Shay's gaze wandered down the length of her new lab partner, Kale Alexander, as he gracefully guided Hooker Barbie around the dimly lit dance floor.

With the exception of herself, the rest of the women in the bridal party hovered in the corner around a plump Christmas tree, clucking like chicks in a henhouse when the rooster strutted in. She couldn't blame them, really. With a hot bod like his, Kale was every woman's fantasy.

If she were a good girl, perhaps Santa would wrap him up and tuck him under her tree. A devious grin that would rival the Grinch's curled her painted lips.

Pinching her eyes shut, she shook her head to clear it from

its delicious meanderings. How in the heck could she be expected to work side by side with that sexy distraction for the next month without losing focus on her task?

She darn well had to find a way because her career advancement at Iowa Research Center hinged on the success of their project. It was time to stop drooling over her temporary lab partner and concentrate on their assignment.

Perched on a stool, she gestured for the bartender to bring another strawberry daiquiri and worked at schooling her wayward thoughts. When the love ballad ended and "Jingle Bell Rock" boomed from a nearby speaker, her curious glance drifted back to Kale, despite a hard-fought battle to look the other away.

Raven black locks that were a tad too long for office standards brushed his collar as he bent forward. Warm tingles rushed through her bloodstream as she imaged how those silky strands would feel caressing her naked flesh. Taking an extra moment to indulge in the erotic slide show, she watched him whisper something into Barbie's ear before backing away.

She noted with mute satisfaction that Hooker Barbie, otherwise known as Deanne Sinclair, a junior research scientist from her department who had fought valiantly for Erin's new lead position, appeared to be quite miffed by his sudden departure. What a pity, Erin mused.

As Kale negotiated his way through the crowd, he shrugged off his tux jacket, tossed it over a broad shoulder, and rolled his cuffs to his elbows. With easy, casual strides that displayed his self-assurance and charisma, he sauntered toward the bar.

Toward her.

As she leisurely admired him from afar, visions of sugarplums danced in her . . .

Wait. Her brain skidded to a halt and backtracked. She drew a breath and tried again. Visions of their assignment to test Pleasure Prolonged, a drug enabling men to have prolonged erections and multiple orgasms, danced in her head.

She smiled. There, that was better. Back on track.

Hell, who was she kidding? Work was the farthest thing from her mind. The man was a walking wet dream, and her skin grew warm every time he came near. Her smile crumbled as her gaze swept over him once again.

Good Lord, if he looked that delectable in a tailored tux, she could only imagine how scrumptious he'd look out of it.

And imagine she did!

Beginning with his linebacker shoulders, she visually undressed him. Every magnificent inch of him. Proceeding from the unbuttoned collar of his form-fitting dress shirt, her gaze began a slow descent. She felt her pulse race as she traced the pattern of his wide chest, sculpted arms, and tight waist. Her inspection halted and lingered at the junction of his impressive muscular thighs.

His black dress pants molded to his legs like hot wax to a candle. Her breath hitched; her pulse raced. Holy Mother of God, he looked as if he were packing a nine iron behind his zipper. The provocative mental image of where she'd like him to sink his next putt flashed through her mind like a lightning storm. A shiver tightened her stomach while a rush of liquid heat dampened her silky panties. She bit back a breathy moan as beads of perspiration dotted her forehead.

If Santa could read her mind now, the only thing under her tree would be a humongous lump of coal.

Sitting under the multicolor strobe light, her whole body vibrated and moistened with indecent images, and for a brief moment she wondered if her flesh glistened like the silvery garland shimmering on the Christmas tree.

Kale's lazy gaze sifted through the crowd and settled on Erin. Ripples of sensual pleasure danced over her skin, inciting tiny goose bumps to pebble her flesh when his piercing blue eyes searched her out. Seconds seemed to crawl into minutes as she held his lingering glance. Enticing lips turned up over perfect white teeth as he flashed her his trademark bad-boy grin, a grin capable of charming the skin off a snake, or the dress off a lascivious maid of honor.

Sucking in a shuddery breath, she linked her fingers together and brushed her tongue over parched lips.

"No doubt about it. With Kale swinging the driver, one thrust would guarantee him a hole in one."

"Excuse me? What was that you just said?"

Damn, she hadn't said that out loud, had she? Erin reluctantly tore her gaze from Kale and twisted around to face the bride. God, the sight of Laura in her wedding gown took Erin's breath away.

Clearing her throat, Erin slanted her head sideways and

tapped her nails on the bar. She furrowed her brow and glared at her best friend in mock annoyance. "Shouldn't you be on your honeymoon by now?"

Laura grinned and ignored the question. She smoothed her fingers over the bodice of her dress. "By the look on your face, I'd say you'll be the next one dressed in white." She leaned forward in her seat, her eyes wide. "Perhaps you'd like to borrow mine."

Erin scoffed, held her hands up in a halting motion, and gave a defiant shake of her head. Tendrils of hair slipped from their moorings and tumbled down her shoulders, coming to rest on her pretty blue, strapless maid-of-honor gown.

"Uh-uh. Forget it. Not me. No way am I going to tie the noose … I mean knot." She rolled her eyes heavenward and cringed like she'd just eaten rancid sushi.

Laura chuckled easily and brushed Erin's hair from her shoulders. Her voice softened. "He who protests the most—"

With a wave of her hand, Erin cut her off and finished the sentence. "Has the weakest argument. I know, I know. But trust me, it's not a path I ever plan on traveling. Men are good for one thing and one thing only. Sex."

Visions of herself walking that path, or rather, church aisle, had been squelched years ago. After coming home early from work one day to retrieve a forgotten file, she'd found her fiancé howling like a hound, going at it doggie style in her bed with his slut secretary. What really pissed her off was that the cheating, lying bastard had felt justified in his actions. He'd been quick to inform her that men had certain expectations and special needs, and not only had she failed to live up to his, he assured her that no man in his right mind would ever put up with her long hours at the research center.

So she'd been working extra shifts at the lab to build her career. Was it a crime to want to focus on her future, to strive for success? One little bump in the road and Dwayne had taken the first exit instead of supporting her when she'd needed it the most.

Since that eye-opening incident, she'd decided she didn't want or need a man in her life. As long as she had her career, she had all she needed. No man was ever going to control how she lived her life, or determine how many hours she spent at the lab pursuing her dream.

Erin pushed a wayward curl from her forehead and pressed her lips into a fine line. "I'm into simple, casual, uncomplicated sex," she said with conviction.

She sighed as the bitter truth dawned on her. Besides her ex-fiancé, Dwayne the Dog, she'd slept with only one other guy. In all honesty, she was all talk and no action. Obviously her strong physical reaction to Kale was her body's not-so-subtle reminder that it was time for a little less conversation and little more action. Good Lord, now she was quoting Elvis. She was in worse shape than she realized.

"A hump and a bump, thank you chump," Erin reinforced. She sank farther into the cushiony seat of the stool and folded her arms across her chest.

"Is that right?" A deep, sexy, masculine voice sounded from behind her. "How interesting. I've never quite heard it put that way before."

Erin spun around, came face-to-face with Kale, and nearly bit off her tongue.

Kale leaned against the bar and let his gaze drift over Erin's soft curves and sculpted angles. He studied her flawless features and took his sweet time to appreciate the exotic beauty before him.

One word came to mind. Exquisite. Billowy nutmeg curls framed her heart-shaped face and tumbled in disarray over the bare flesh of her delicate shoulders. A sexy pink flush bloomed high on her cheeks, and he fought the impulse to caress her, to see if her face felt warm to the touch.

He regarded her for a quiet, thoughtful moment, wondering if that seductive blush inching its way over the silky column of her neck would travel all the way out to the peaks of her well-rounded breasts. Breasts that had been coloring his dreams, as well as his every waking thought, since he'd shared a dozen or so cramped car rides with her over the last week as they traveled to and from the prewedding activities.

"Casual, uncomplicated sex." Nodding in agreement, Kale echoed her sentiments and raised an inquisitive brow. "Is there any other kind?"

Erin's pretty pink tongue darted out to moisten plump, cinnamon-painted lips.

Cinnamon. His favorite. He'd spent countless hours fantasizing about smothering those smooth lips of hers with his own to see if they tasted as sweet as they looked. His muscles bunched and pulsed in heated anticipation as fire pitched through him. Well, at least one muscle in particular.

Locking her arms more tightly over her chest, she said, "Not to me." She gave a defiant tilt of her head, but for a fleeting second he detected conflicting emotions in her expressive brown eyes. Her breathing hitched and she broke eye contact with him. With her long black lashes fluttering nervously, she glanced around the room, looking everywhere but at his face.

Her bizarre reaction didn't escape him. Her nervous gestures and body language spoke volumes. Erin Shay wasn't as nonchalant about sex as she led everyone to believe.

Erin unlocked her arms and exhaled what appeared to be a relieved breath when the bartender arrived with her drink. Clearly no longer wishing to pursue their conversation, she twirled on her stool, leaned forward, and wrapped her fingers around the wide, frosty glass. With an innocent sensuality that aroused all his senses and rocketed his hormones into hyper speed, she poised the pink straw inches from her glossy mouth and parted her delectable lips.

Christ, he really wished she hadn't done that.

Kale gulped and felt his blood rush at the sight of her luscious mouth and fleshy lips. Lips designed for kissing.

Him.

Everywhere.

Now.

Pleasure Prolonged

Fuck!

Her tongue snaked out and drew the straw inside. Puckering her mouth, she took a long suck, mirrored a sexy bedroom purr, and swallowed the icy concoction.

Desire twisted inside him as a burst of heat shot straight to his groin, making it tighten painfully. He suspected this woman had no idea how sexy she was or that she'd been getting under his skin for the past week. Hell, since the minute he'd looked into her seductive eyes, the attraction was instant, potent, all-consuming, and anything but casual. There was no denying how much he wanted her. And right now the sight of her wet, sensuous lips wrapped around that long, tubular straw filled his mind with all kinds of wild and wicked images.

Kale eased himself onto a stool and draped his tux jacket over his lap. He angled closer, close enough to breathe in her arousing feminine scent. His nostrils flared as her hypnotic aroma curled around him and seeped under his skin. She smelled like a fragrant spring flower on a warm sunny day. Heaven help him, he'd make a deal with the devil himself to be the bumblebee in charge of pollinating that blossom.

He exhaled an agonized groan and clenched his jaw. If he didn't banish his thoughts and curb his desires, his jacket would soon be performing a magical hovering act.

When she swirled on her stool, their outer thighs connected. Lust clawed its way to the surface and clamored for attention. A thin sheen of moisture dampened his skin. The soft scrape of her silky smooth leg against his drove every sane thought from his passion-rattled brain.

Without fully considering his actions, he reached out and brushed a tendril of nutmeg hair from her delicate shoulder.

Would the silky curls at the apex of her legs be the same buttery soft texture, the same rich color?

Surprise registered on her face, and she flinched at his intimate touch. Her warm hand darted out and closed over his. The sweet friction of skin rubbing skin made his cock pulse and thicken.

Twining a wavy curl around his finger, his hand hovered near the creamy swell of her full cleavage for an extra second. Long enough for him to absorb the heat radiating from her naked flesh. Gorgeous chocolate, come-hither eyes stared at him in utter shock.

She shivered under his invasive touch. "What are you doing?" Erin asked. Her tone might have sounded alarmed, but the spark igniting her eyes told an entirely different story.

Wondering what color the soft tuft of curly hair between your thighs would be if you were drenched with passion.

Pulling his hand away, he swallowed. Hard. Like he had a dry piece of steak lodged in his throat.

"Your hair was about to dip into your drink." *And I was about to come on the spot.* He felt it best to keep that last thought to himself.

"Oh." She blew her wispy bangs off her forehead. With lips close enough to taste, her sweet, strawberry-scented breath wafted across his face. His mouth salivated, eager for a deeper, more satisfying taste. A fever rose in him. He had no idea what kind of spell she had over him, but he wanted her with a passion he'd never before experienced.

As she ran her finger around the perimeter of her glass, his thoughts fragmented. How could she make such an innocent movement so damn erotic? He shifted to alleviate the tight ache in his groin.

"Thanks," she murmured, her voice dropping an octave. "You'd think my hair had a mind of its own." Her low chuckle sounded rough, edgy. She brushed a few loose strands from her shoulder and grinned. "So much for sitting under the dryer for hours." Rolling her eyes, she lifted one slender shoulder and gave a resigned sigh. "That's why I usually skip the salon and pull it back into a ponytail."

"Fancy hairstyles don't really fit you, do they, Erin?" He liked that about her. She was perky, earthy, natural, and beautiful without high-priced hairstyles and layers of makeup.

It occurred to him that Erin was the antithesis of the women from his social circle in Los Angeles, superficial women caring only about their needs and desires while pretending to have depth and empathy for others. After spending the last week around Erin, Kale could see right through her bad-girl act. He caught glimpses of a woman who was full of warmth and compassion pretending to be superficial, something his every instinct told him she wasn't.

How interesting.

"I noticed you always wore your hair tied back during rehearsals." He gave a slow nod and paused to consider her a moment longer. "It suits you. I liked it that way."

She laughed in response and shot him a wary look. The low, throaty, bewitching sound of her aphrodisiacal tone rolled over him.

One perfect eyebrow arched. "That's a first. I always thought men liked a woman's hair long and loose, so they could run their hands through it." Wiggling her fingers, she mimicked the actions.

A casual shrug curled his shoulders. Shutting out the din of the crowd, he lowered his voice and nestled closer. He pressed his body against hers and put his mouth near her ear. "Yes, well, I guess I'm not like most men."

A doubtful expression crossed her face but she didn't respond. Breaking contact, she twisted sideways, pursed her lips, and took another long suck from her straw.

Hell, those plump lips of hers looked like they were begging to be kissed.

His dick sprang higher, as though hoping to glimpse the woman who was causing all the southern commotion. Fuck. His twenty-one-gun salute had just blown his ability to stand for the next ten minutes or so. Unless he wanted everyone in the room to know he was sporting the mother of all boners, he'd have to remain seated. He closed his eyes in distress and muttered curses of sexual frustration under his breath.

Before his control completely obliterated, he redirected his thoughts and called on a cock-taming trick he'd learned back in junior high school. He thought of football, basketball, soccer, anything with balls. Damn, that wasn't working. He had balls. And right now they were in a goddamn uproar.

As his mind drifted back to the gorgeous woman beside him, his dick refused to cooperate. *Step aside, Houdini, and make room for the amazing Kale Alexander and his gravity-defying jacket.*

The groom, Jay, came up beside Laura. Kale adjusted his coat, thankful for the distraction. He cleared his throat and shook his head, hoping to lift the fog from his lust-filled mind.

"Time to toss the bouquet," Jay said, wrapping his hands around Laura's waist in a protective manner that had Laura's eyes brimming with the love she felt for him.

Laura planted a warm kiss on Jay's mouth and slid from her stool. Kale still found it hard to believe that "Wildman" Jay Cutler had finally settled down and gotten married. Although, in all honesty, he had to admit that he'd never seen his best friend happier.

As Kale watched the loving couple for a moment longer, he acknowledged the pang of envy that rushed over him and sat heavy in his heart. It left a hollow, empty feeling in the pit of his stomach.

Six months previous, a surprise phone call from his best friend, Jay, announcing his engagement and asking Kale to be his best man, had acted as a catalyst for Kale, causing him to pause and consider the path of his own future and his playboy lifestyle.

Now, being back in his hometown, around his family, old friends, and familiar surroundings, made him realize how truly discontented he was with living in Los Angeles. Years ago a university scholarship had sent him west with promises of happiness and financial success. He'd found only the latter. Becoming the head of the research and development wing at Castech Research Center, Iowa Research Center's parent company, had given him the financial security he'd strived for, but his playboy, bachelor lifestyle no longer brought him happiness. In fact, it left him feeling restless and unfulfilled.

Kale's gaze swept across the room, acknowledging all the familiar faces. Packing up and leaving everything behind to journey to the coast hadn't been easy for him, but he knew he had no choice. His father's death fifteen years before had left him shouldering the responsibility of his younger sisters. Since his mother's secretarial job barely put food on the table, Kale knew the position in Los Angeles would afford him the funds needed to help take care of her household finances and put his two younger sisters through college.

Although Kale enjoyed his position at Castech, he'd come to understand Los Angeles wasn't a place where he wanted to settle down for a lifetime and raise a family. And he definitely wanted a family. Now he was just waiting for the right woman to come along. One who stirred him physically and emotionally, and who shared the same values and beliefs. Up until a week ago, he had begun to question whether such a woman existed.

Laura slipped her arm around Erin's shoulder. "Come on. Time for you to catch a bouquet."

"No way," Erin protested, shrugging away. She sliced one hand through the air, her voice elevating an octave. "There are plenty of single females here who'd die to catch it. I'm not one of them." She planted her feet on the rung of her stool. A spirited fire burned in her dark brown eyes as a pink tinge colored her cheeks.

When Erin spotted the determined look in Laura's eyes, she angled her chin in defiance. "Forget it, Laura—" Her words died away when Jay swiftly removed her drink from her hand.

Laura winked at Jay. "Thank you, honey."

Giving her no reprieve, Laura hauled Erin from the stool and dragged her to the dance floor. Kale grinned and watched the action with mute fascination.

Where the hell was an arena full of mud when you needed it?

"What's the matter with you?"

The sound of Jay's voice broke his concentration. "What?" Kale twisted sideways to face his best friend and wiped the smirk from his mouth.

Furrowing his brow, Jay scrutinized Kale and signaled the bartender. "If your tongue hung any lower you'd be tripping on it. I've never seen you so distracted by a woman before." Jay accepted two cold beers and handed one to Kale.

Kale rolled his tongue back into his dry mouth, grunted something incoherent, and drained half the bitter liquor in one gulp. Much better. Now if only he could soak one other body part in the amber elixir.

Ignoring the discomfort pulling at his ever-tightening groin, he took another long haul from the bottle. Fuck, he needed a cold shower. Either that or he was going to find himself in a tug-of-war with the palm twins when he got home. His palms. A home remedy guaranteed to relieve tension and reduce swelling.

"She's a ball breaker, Kale," Jay warned. "Not your type at all."

Kale's bottle hit the bar with a thud. "Yeah? You think so?"

Jay scoffed. "I know so," he said with certainty. "I've seen her in action."

Kale had his suspicions. There was something about her that led him to believe otherwise. He sensed a vulnerability about her that she took great pains to guard. Gut instinct told him the bad-girl act was just that. An act. A facade. One he suspected she was interested in exploring further. Damned if he, and only he, was going to be the one to help her along with that journey. And in the process he was going to get to know her on a deeper level and show her that sex between them would be anything but casual.

"You have no idea what you're getting yourself into." Jay shook his head and patted Kale on the back. "She's a man-eater. She'll chew you up and spit you out, pal."

A slow grin curled Kale's mouth. "That's what I'm counting on."

Chapter 2

Erin reluctantly gave up struggling and let Laura escort her to the dance floor. "Okay, Laura you win. You can let go of me now," she blurted, seconds before her breasts popped out of her tight bodice.

Laura released Erin's arm, leaned close, and whispered into her ear, "Are you and Kale going to test Pleasure Prolonged on yourselves?"

Erin's mouth curved. Wouldn't that be the perfect opportunity to take a stab at being the bad girl she pretended to be and give her libidinous body the action it craved? Shame they already had test subjects lined up for Monday morning's experiment.

She looked at her friend, hoping her face conveyed nonchalance about the whole issue.

"No. We never discussed it." Her gazed moved across

the room and settled on Kale. A fine tremor rippled over her flesh as she watched him watching her.

"Why not?" Laura probed. "I hear he's into casual sex." Laura winked at her. "Just your type."

Erin held out her index finger and puckered her lips. "First, he's not my type." *Liar.* She'd have to be comatose not to stand up and take notice of him. Even then, she wasn't so sure that would stop her. His mere presence would likely rouse any woman from a coma. Probably a few men too. Her middle finger joined the first. "And second, I really need to concentrate on this assignment. As you know, my career advancement depends on it."

Concentrate! Ha! Like that was going to happen. There'd be no concentrating going on with him around. Maybe she should just have sex with him. *Casual sex. Uncomplicated sex.* To get him out of her system, or into her system, she mused, depending on which way you looked at it. Perhaps then she'd be able to get her mind off her libido and back on her job.

She paused to give that last thought further consideration. She'd never had a one-night stand before. *Would it be possible for her to indulge in a frivolous affair with a gorgeous, smart playboy like Kale, a guy who stirred all her senses, without threatening her emotions?*

Some deeper instinct warned her that sex with him would be anything *but* uncomplicated.

"And third," she continued. "After you and Jay secretly

tested the libido suppressant on one another without consent, Kale and I have been duly warned by the director. If we step out of line, it will cost us our jobs."

Laura looked far from convinced but didn't press the issue. Instead, she turned and made her way to the raised platform at the front of the dance stage while Erin padded across the floor to the far back.

Just because she was forced to stand there with all the other eager, single women didn't mean she had to catch the damn bouquet. She could neatly sidestep it and let Hooker Barbie jump for the coveted flowers. The blond bombshell looked like a crouched tiger waiting to pounce on a gazelle. Scary. Erin gave a mock shiver, and under the guise of fearing for her safety, circled Barbie, keeping a wide berth.

She found a nice, quiet spot in the corner and turned her attention to the man on the other side of the room. Kale and Jay were deep in conversation. From the intent look on Kale's face, she assumed it was an extremely important topic. As Erin pondered what issue they were discussing, something soft and fragrant hit her square in the chest. Her hands automatically reached out, and before she realized it, she was holding the bouquet.

Erin mumbled curses under her breath. Forget the judge and jury, Laura was headed straight for execution!

Earlier in the evening, Kale had had no intention of participating in the traditional garter toss. Rather interesting that he now found himself standing front and center on the dance floor, the most prominent position for catching the lacy slip of blue material.

He shot Erin a sidelong glance. Perched on a stool, she brushed her silky nutmeg hair from her face as her gaze darted around the room. Nervous anticipation danced in her big, dark eyes as she absentmindedly twirled a wayward lock around her finger.

Kale's attention drifted back to Jay in time to watch him exchange a look with Laura. A moment later the blue lace sailed right into his open palm. He twisted sideways to glimpse the sexy woman who made him feel like a lustful teenager on his first date. Her sensuous mouth opened and closed in a silent gasp. He could almost hear the air rush from her lungs in a whoosh. Kale widened his stance and watched her for a moment longer. He had to admit, he was looking forward to discovering the woman behind the role she played.

The lights on the dance floor dimmed as Jay came up beside him and patted him on the back. "Play nice."

Kale raked his hair off his forehead and chuckled. "I always play nice. Hard, but nice." With the crook of his finger, he motioned for Erin to come to him.

Pulling her dress high on her long legs, she slipped her curvy backside off her seat and met his gaze unflinchingly. His glance left her face and slowly perused the length of her. Languorous warmth stole through him as he envisioned himself sliding the garter over her slim calf all the way up to her shapely, sexy thigh.

With casual aplomb she sauntered closer and accepted a chair in the center of the dance floor.

The soft golden glow of the shadowy overhead light made her skin glisten. Her flowery scent stirred the air around them, leaving him feeling slightly light-headed. Erotic dance music began playing in the background while cheers originated in the crowd.

Shutting out the noise of the audience, Kale dropped to his knees, insinuated himself between her legs, and gripped the hem of her dress. Her body fairly vibrated. He leaned in close. His mouth was mere inches from her ear. "Do you mind?" he whispered.

Her breath stalled as she shook her head. One perfect eyebrow rose a fraction. "Why would I mind?" she asked, her voice deceptively controlled, but her shaky breathing betrayed her emotions.

He shrugged and pitched his voice low. "Just thought I'd ask. I'm not one to presume anything." He curled the fabric of her dress in his hand and moved in closer. "I'd never touch a woman who didn't want my touch."

She opened her mouth to speak, hesitated, swiped her tongue over her bottom lip and then slid it shut. Damn that mouth. So plump. So luscious. This woman got to him the way no other woman ever had.

"Tell me something, Erin." He pulled her dress up higher, until he exposed the sleek curve of her inner thighs. His nostrils flared as he visually caressed her. "Do you want my touch?"

Slender shoulders lifted. "I …" She stumbled over that one word. He could almost hear her mind racing. Her hesitation lasted only seconds, then something in her expression changed.

His gaze latched on to her breasts as she straightened her back and drew air deep into her lungs. She flung a wayward curl from her forehead and met his gaze straight on.

Even though there wasn't a trace of uncertainty in her expression, he glimpsed a guarded looked in her eyes before she quickly blinked it away. Kale knew she wanted to test unexplored waters and experiment with another side of herself, and he wanted to help her with that, but he also sensed her unease. A surge of tenderness rushed over him as his protective instincts kicked into high gear. He looked deep into her eyes, letting her know she was in the right hands.

"Yes, I want your touch."

A primitive growl full of male prowess sounded low in his throat. "Good. Because I want to touch you."

Oblivious to everyone around him, he removed her satin shoe and eased the lace over her silk stocking. With a feathery light caress, his hand began a lazy journey up her calf. She immediately reacted to his intimate touch. The sound of her indrawn breath pleased him. Her warm and wanting flesh began to quiver as a fragment of her control dissipated.

"Mmmm," he moaned. "You have beautiful legs, Erin." His voice dripped with desire. The cheering of the crowd faded into the background as he focused his entire concentration on her.

Pleasure Prolonged

A light dusting of pink colored her cheeks as she inched her thighs open wider, providing him with easier access. When she moistened her lips, saliva pooled on his tongue. Fuck, did she know how irresistible that mouth was? He became acutely aware of how much he ached to plunder her lush sweetness.

She made a sexy sound and shifted. "Thanks." There was a slight tremor in her voice.

As his fingers slid over her smooth calf, she took a gulping breath. Her sweet responses urged him on and filled him with raw, primitive desire.

"Something tells me Jay and Laura planned for us to end up together like this." Lust swamped him, deepening his voice, making it barely recognizable.

Her sexy, nervous laugh seeped into his skin, evoking a shudder from his body. His muscles bunched as perspiration beaded on his forehead.

"I think you're right." She dipped her head to meet his glance. Dark eyes brimmed with desire as they met. "Since we're both into *casual* sex, Laura thought it would be a good idea to test Pleasure Prolonged on each other," she said, gauging his reactions carefully.

He mulled over that idea for quite some time. Although the idea sounded intriguing, and it would be the perfect opportunity to ease his painful, week-long hard-on, something told him the tests would be less than accurate. Besides, he didn't want Erin to have sex with him under those terms. He wanted her to come to him on her own. And he didn't want it to be casual.

When he didn't immediately respond, she rushed on. "That way we'd be sure of the results and wouldn't have to rely on test subjects or machine readouts."

Frowning intently, he furrowed his brow and pressed his lips into a fine line. "I don't think that's such a great idea. We'd never be able to test the drug on each other."

A crestfallen expression crossed her face. She lowered her gaze to the floor. Kale nudged her chin up. "I'm afraid the formula would be wasted on me, Erin."

The confusion she felt was evident in her eyes. "What do you mean?" Then suddenly, as if confusion made its way to understanding, she flinched, her mouth forming a perfect circle.

"Are you gay?" she blurted out.

He stifled a chuckle. She was so damn cute.

She closed her eyes and shook her head in dismay. "Why are all the gorgeous ones gay?"

So she thought he was gorgeous, did she? He lifted his lips in a half smile. "You see, Erin, if I buried my cock inside your sweetness, I'm bound to have a prolonged erection and multiple orgasms. No drugs needed," he said, letting her know exactly how he felt about her.

"Oh," she mumbled, her voice tight. She bit her lip and flushed darker. He watched her throat work as she swallowed.

Even though they were practically draped in darkness, he wanted to ensure their privacy. He pulled her dress to her calves, obscuring the crowd's vision and blocking his actions. His hands trailed higher, until they were a hairbreadth away from the heat of her desire. He wondered how she'd react if he grazed her silk-covered cleft. Wondered what kind of sound she'd make if they were alone and he lapped at her with his tongue. Would she purr? Moan? Mewl?

He stroked her flesh and toyed with the wide band on her stockings. The look on her face told him all he needed to know. His touch aroused her. That pleased the hell out of him. He kept a telltale smile from his mouth. Kale knew he'd never wanted a woman to want him as much as he did tonight. He'd certainly felt powerful sexual desire before, but never this potent.

Her breath came in a low rush. "Kale ..." she whispered as his fingers feathered over her thighs.

Her hypnotic tone pulled him under. When he met her glance, electricity crackled between them. Plump lips parted as her heat reached out to him.

"Yeah?" he asked.

Watching her squirm in her seat filled him with erotic visions of how her sexy body would move underneath him. Christ, there was nothing he wanted more than to pin her hands above her head and feel her writhing and gyrating beneath him. His pulse raced in a mad cadence as he relished the arousing image.

Her tongue made a slow pass over her bottom lip. With a slight nod, she gestured to his hand as he moved the garter higher on her thigh. "That tickles," she murmured.

He lifted a brow. "Then I guess that means I'm doing it right."

Her eyes clouded with need. "Something tells me you always do it right, Kale," she breathed into his mouth.

He grinned and pitched his voice low. "I've never had any complaints yet."

She drew her bottom lip between her teeth and lowered her voice to match his. "Are we still talking about putting on a garter?"

His grin turned wicked. "Not even for a minute."

She flushed darker. "I didn't think so." Her soft tone made him weak with need.

His body trembled almost uncontrollably. As her heat curled around him, all he could think about was how he'd like to take her home and satisfy her in ways she'd never been satisfied before.

If he hadn't promised his family he'd be there for their ritual Sunday dinner, he'd scoop Erin up, haul her back to his place, and let her experiment with the role of bad girl as he made sweet love to her all weekend long until work beckoned them Monday morning.

He ached to lock himself deep inside her while he explored her curves and traced the pattern of her body with his fingers and his tongue. He wanted to lave her nipples with long, luxurious strokes and suck on her hard buds until she became feverish with need and came completely apart in his arms. He wanted to look deep into her soulful, warm brown eyes and watch her lose the control that she so painfully guarded as she reached a powerful, earth-shattering climax.

Although this wasn't the time or the place for such intimacy, the situation was escalating beyond his power to stop it. At this particular moment, his head ruled his actions. Unfortunately, it was the swollen, hormone-driven head pressing insistently against its zippered cage that demanded undivided attention.

Curious hands climbed higher. His forward motion was thwarted when his fingers reached the apex between her legs.

Heat radiated from her sex and warmed his body. The seductive, feminine tang of her arousal reached his nostrils. He inhaled her heady aroma and sensed that her needs and desires matched his own.

He felt dampness on her silk panties and could barely summon the strength to speak. He stroked her. Softly. Barely touching her nether lips.

Holy fuck. She was drenched. His mind stopped working.

She tensed against him and gasped. Her hips jerked forward, driving his fingers harder against her cleft as she leaned into him. Her shaky hand intercepted his. Kale sensed it was a token gesture to stop him. The ardent darkening of her eyes and her body language belied her actions.

With their lips mere inches apart, she whispered in a hushed tone, *"Kale?"* Her voice was far from steady.

"Look up," he managed to say around the lump forming in his throat.

Her eyes were dark, glossy, perplexed. She frowned in concentration. "What?"

He drew a deep, fortifying breath and nestled his face

close to her perfumed neck. Her sweet scented skin nearly shut down his brain.

He slipped a finger under her chin. "Look up, Erin, and tell me what you see."

She tilted her head and squinted in the dim light. Her dark brows knitted together as her chest rose and fell with her quick breathing. Kale felt his tongue go dry at the sight of her long, pale neck. He watched her pulse jump at the base of her throat. That's where he wanted his mouth. Right where her creamy neck melted into her collarbone.

She went absolutely still when she spotted a thick cluster of green leaves. Her head descended ever so slowly. Lust and something else, something that looked like raw, unbridled need, touched her eyes as they met his.

"Mistletoe ..." Her breathless voice was nothing more than a faint whisper.

"Do you mind if I kiss you?"

She parted her lips, but before she could say anything further, he took possession of her mouth. Moaning, her tongue snaked out and tangled with his. He could taste her sweetness on her strawberry-soaked tongue.

She was so responsive. So damn responsive. He could only imagine how she'd be when he got her alone. Which had to be soon, otherwise his body was going to explode into a million fragments.

He barely had time to explore her entire mouth when she eased away and broke the kiss. The sound of the crowd brought him back to his senses.

He leaned back on his heels and gazed at her. So beautiful. The gentleman in him urged him to apologize for ravishing her in public. But truthfully, the only thing he was sorry for was that he couldn't finish what he started and bring her body to the heights of passion he suspected she craved.

She drew a deep, calming breath. Her voice was low, sexy. "I knew you were into casual sex, Kale, but you failed to warn me you liked to get intimate in public places." She looked down shyly and curled the hem of her dress around her index finger. "I believe I was unprepared."

She was anything but unprepared, and there was nothing casual about what they had just experienced. Whether she believed it or not. It had stirred him emotionally, warmed him right down to his toes, and left him yearning for more. Definitely a feeling he'd never encountered before.

He grinned. His eyes moved over her face. "Meet me in an elevator sometime and I'll show you how much I like public places."

Her head snapped up. She shivered almost violently.

Kale sensed it was a shiver of anticipation.

Chapter 3

A light dusting of snow fell over Kale's much too flashy candy-apple red rental truck as he pulled into his mother's circular driveway. Strings of white icicle lights lined the perimeter of the aged cedar-shingled bungalow and twinkled in the dark night. Kale smiled. For as long as he could remember, his mother had always made Christmas a special time for her three children, regardless of their limited funds.

A sense of belonging washed over him as he took a moment to peruse his old neighborhood. Not much had changed since he left eight years ago. He'd been home for visits, of course, but this was the first time he'd been back for the holidays. Earlier in the week, he'd spent time with his mother, but now he was looking forward to catching up with his sisters and spending Christmas as a family, instead of waking up in his overpriced condo with some corporate climber who was nothing more to him than a passing interest. Nor was he anything more to her.

Kale knew his reputation as a playboy had preceded him. It was a well-known fact that he'd played the bachelor game and lived the playboy lifestyle, just like all the other men and women in his social circle. Six months ago, after realizing he wanted more out of life, he'd begun searching for a woman who stirred him both physically and emotionally. He'd almost given up his quest to find his perfect partner.

Almost.

Now, after meeting a sexy scientist who'd turned his world upside down in the span of a week, he wasn't interested in going back to his old ways and was eager to leave his playboy persona behind him.

Even though Erin had so blatantly stated that men were good for one thing and one thing only—sex—Kale was seeking more from her than a frivolous one-night stand. The first time he set eyes on her, he'd felt like he'd been sucker punched. Her killer smile, intelligence, quick wit, and easy demeanor had him reconsidering his disbelief in love at first sight.

Kale blew out a heavy sigh, knowing Erin wasn't ready to hear him express his feelings and tell her he wasn't simply interested in exploring a brief affair. Gut instinct warned he'd scare her off with his candor. She was guarded and vulnerable for a reason, a reason he vowed to get to the bottom of.

Kale swept his gaze across the small bungalow once again as a movement behind the bay window caught his attention. He'd managed to make a life for himself in Los Angeles, but he had to admit, there was no place like home. It had been far too long since he'd joined the family for one of their ritual Sunday night dinners.

The sound of a car pulling in behind him roused him from his musings. He grabbed his keys from the ignition and reached for his door handle.

Waving wildly, his younger sister Lisa scrambled from the passenger side of the vehicle and dashed toward him. He barely had time to climb out of the driver's seat before she threw her slender arms around his shoulders and squeezed him with a strength someone as tiny as she was couldn't possibly possess.

"Kale," she squealed, her warm breath visible in the chilly night air. "I've missed you."

"Jesus, I can tell," he teased, hugging her back. "Have you been working out?"

Lisa chuckled. "Yeah, Nick works in the campus weight room. He got me hooked."

The wind picked up as Kale gripped her shoulders and inched back. Snow swirled around them and clung to their coats like dander. Kale blinked the heavy wet flakes from his eyelashes and dipped his head to meet his sister's gaze.

"Nick?" he asked, giving her a stern look. His protective instincts surged to the surface. He furrowed his brow and let out a sigh. "Why is this the first I've heard of Nick?"

She whacked him with her gloved hand, sending snow-flakes flying through the air in a mad flurry, and then rubbed her palms together to create heat as the temperature around them dropped a few more degrees.

"Because I didn't need a lecture over the phone and I don't need it now." She waved for Nick to come over.

Kale glanced past his shoulders. As Nick moved toward him, he absorbed every detail of the plow truck who had caught his sister's attention and had given her Schwarzenegger muscles.

Even though he was twice Kale's size, he looked afraid. Good, Kale mused. He should be.

Kale widened his stance and put on his best scowl as the man drew near.

Lisa squeezed his arm in warning. "Kale, stop it. You've scared enough of my boyfriends away over the years. And you can stop protecting me. I'm all grown up."

He cocked a skeptical brow. "All grown up? What are you, twelve now?"

She swatted him. "Very funny. I'm twenty-two and you know it. And I only have one semester left of college." She tilted her chin and flashed him a perfect smile. "Thanks to Jay's connections, I've already got my foot in the door down at Iowa Research Center." Her eyes lit up. "Maybe we'll get to work together someday."

Kale returned her smile. It was nice that Jay had continued to watch over Kale's family in his absence.

Nick moved in beside Lisa and wrapped one arm around her in a protective manner, warming her shivering body, as he thrust his other in Kale's direction. "Nice to meet you, Kale. Lisa has told me so much about you," he said, his voice genuine and sincere as he gave a quick nod of greeting.

Kale gripped the man's thick hand and noted that he had a strong, firm handshake. Kale had always been a good judge of character, and Nick's handshake and direct eye contact spoke volumes. He studied Nick for a moment longer, assessing him. The plow truck's concern for his sister's well-being was evident in the way he rubbed his beefy hand up and down her arm, offering his warmth. Kale noted with an equal measure of surprise and respect that the guy had enough balls to even touch his little sister in front of him. Maybe she'd found herself one of the good guys. Someone who was willing to go against his own best interests to put her needs and desires first.

"And she's told me nothing about you," Kale countered, turning his scowl on his sister. Just then the front door of the bungalow swung open and his mother's voice sounded over the wind.

"Come in here you three, before you catch your death of cold," Grace called out.

Kale chuckled and threw his arm around his sister's waist. "And you think I'm overprotective. Come on. Let's go. I'm starving."

The aroma of freshly baked shortbread cookies reached his nostrils and brought back memories of his youth as he stepped inside. Life hadn't always been easy after their father's sudden heart attack fifteen years ago. Working part-time, maintaining his grades, and shouldering the responsibility of his two younger sisters over the years had been challenging to say the least.

He shrugged his coat off, draped it over the wooden stair rail, and inhaled the delectable scents coming from the kitchen. Jenna, his youngest sister, met him at the door.

As he studied his sister he realized things had changed drastically since his last visit. Dressed entirely in black, with spiked hair to match and a choker chain that resembled a dog collar, Jenna punched him on the shoulder. "Hey bro."

How charming.

He dipped his head to meet her gaze. "Hey Jenna," he returned. Cocking his head, he regarded her for an extra moment. He shoved his hands deep into his pockets, resisting the urge to rip that piercing out of her eyebrow. "How's your last year of high school working out for you? Have you decided on a college yet?"

She gave a very unladylike snort, and then grunted something incoherent before she sauntered back into the living room. Kale turned to his mother and arched a questioning brow.

"What—"

Her palms out, his mother's blue eyes glistened as she cut him off. "It's just another stage. You all went through them. She'll get over it." Grace pushed back her silvery hair and gestured with a nod. "Now come on, dinner is getting cold." Waving her hands, she herded them all to the dining room table.

Following his mother down the short hallway, Kale couldn't manage to tamp down his concerns. He knew at times he could be overprotective, too controlling of those he cared about, but it was that control that had gotten them through the rough times. And there had been many rough times over the years.

Kale moved into the cozy dining room and inhaled the familiar scents of his mother's home cooking. Listening to a Bing Crosby Christmas carol coming from the living room stereo, he lowered himself onto a plush dining room chair and perused his childhood home, orienting himself.

Homemade Christmas decorations adorned every wall while linen Santa placemats and matching napkins covered the old oaken table. He noted how his condo seemed so sterile, so cold in comparison. In all honesty, he didn't spend a lot of time there. When he wasn't waking up in some passing interest's bed, he was at the lab. Lately, however, he acknowledged that most of his nights were spent at the research center, not between some woman's silky sheets.

Of course, his current probationary status at the center was a direct result of the late hours he kept. He'd fucked up. Plain and simple. Late one night in a haze of exhaustion, he'd fallen asleep on the old cot in the back of his lab and had forgotten to lock up. Because of his carelessness, a couple of vials of the serum that he and his team had been working on had gone missing. It could have cost him his job. By all rights it should have. The only thing that saved his ass was that his boss had a soft spot for him, right in the middle of her mattress. But he'd been duly warned, regardless of his impeccable work ethic, that if he fucked up again, at Castech or during his stint at the subsidiary center in Iowa, he could kiss his career good-bye.

Jenna plunked herself down on his left. The movement pulled him back to the present. Lisa and Nick grabbed the seat across the table facing him. As they all situated themselves, Kale uncorked the wine and filled the glasses as his mother brought in the last serving dish and took her seat at the end of the table.

Kale's stomach growled. "It all looks great," he said, his mouth salivating for a home-cooked meal.

His mother grinned at the endorsement. "Yes, well, I have to fatten you up. You're looking too thin."

Kale scoffed at the remark. Damn, he kept himself in great shape. In fact, he worked out regularly at the health club. But if you were comparing him to the plow truck on the other side of the table, well, hell yeah, he looked thin. Anyone would.

As his mother's gaze fixed on him, her eyes softened. Kale could only imagine what was running through her mind, visions of a daughter-in-law and the splendor of a child's laughter in the house once again. He'd heard those comments numerous times over the last few years, but the timing had never been right before. He'd been far too busy striving for success and living the playboy lifestyle. But now that he'd encountered a sweet, fiery woman who turned his world upside down, all that had changed.

"What you need is a wife to cook for you," she added. "Surely you must have found a nice woman out west."

Kale smiled at her old-fashioned ways as he thought about the corporate climbers he'd dated in Los Angeles.

Superficial women who were quick to take from him, yet
never eager to give anything in return. Women pretending
to be something they weren't. He couldn't imagine any one
of them ever cooking for herself, let alone for him. In fact,
he was the one who'd always done all the cooking. Not that
he minded; he enjoyed being in the kitchen. And soon, very
soon, he hoped he'd be preparing breakfast in bed for one
very special lady.

As his thoughts journeyed to the sexy scientist who
evoked unfamiliar feelings in him, a sudden burst of warmth
streaked through his body and reverberated through his
blood. It amazed him how just thinking of Erin could rouse
such intense emotions. There was something about her that
pulled at him. She'd gotten under his skin without even
trying. No woman had ever affected him that way.

Kale's whole life had been about shouldering responsibility and taking care of others. He'd never been selfish or
put his needs first. Now, for the first time, he was about to
do something just for him. With single-minded determination, he was going to go after what he wanted. And he wasn't
going to stop until he broke through Erin's defenses and had
her writhing beneath him on his bed.

Lisa's voice jolted him out of his thoughts. "Yeah, big
brother, when are you going to get yourself a good old-
fashioned woman to cook for you?"

Kale kicked her under the table. Without breaking her
smile, she kicked him back. Hard. It damn well hurt. Just
like old times, he mused.

"Tell me, Nick. What do you do besides train my scrawny sister at the gym?" he prompted with a smile.

Jenna chuckled in response to his question. The joyous sound made Kale smile. It pleased him to catch a glimpse of the playful young girl he'd left behind eight years ago.

Nick cleared his throat. "I'm in my senior year of physiotherapy. I want to work with sports injuries."

Impressive.

"If all goes well, after graduation I'll be working at the clinic a block away from Lisa." Nick lowered his head and smiled as his gaze collided with Lisa's. "We'll be able to have lunch together every day," Nick added.

Kale felt a lump clog his throat as the two exchanged a long, lingering look. It occurred to him that the plow truck really and truly loved his sister.

"What about you Kale, are you just passing through?" Nick asked.

Jenna piped in. "Or are you home to stay this time?" The eager tone in her voice gained his attention. Her hand closed over his and squeezed.

Kale twisted to face his youngest sister. He spotted a gleam of hope in her wide blue eyes as she handed him a bowl full of mashed potatoes. The look on her face caught him by surprise. He hadn't realized just how much his baby sister had missed him, how much his absence over the years had affected her. Jenna had been only a toddler when they lost their dad, and Kale had been the only father figure she'd ever known. His heart tightened in his chest.

Cathryn Fox

"You could probably get on full-time at the research center," Jenna continued, adjusting the spiked bracelets on her wrist, enabling her to delve into her meal.

Kale helped himself to a heaping spoonful of potatoes and passed the bowl on. It wasn't the first time since he'd been back that he'd considered that option. The pay wouldn't be as high, but then again, he no longer needed it to be. Lisa would be out of college in a few months, and he had enough money tucked away to take care of Jenna's education. It really would be nice to be closer to his family. Jenna certainly looked as though she could use some male influence. And he'd have to keep an eye on the plow truck to make sure he treated his sister properly. Kale suspected wedding bells would be ringing in their near future.

At the mere notion of wedding bells, his thoughts careened backward in time to relive the passionate kiss he'd shared with Erin at Jay and Laura's reception. A kiss so full of emotion and tenderness it nearly brought him to his knees.

Casual, his ass!

Hell, no woman could possibly kiss like that without feeling some deeper connection.

Erin's arousing feminine scent and the slow, torturous way her tongue had mated with his while he explored her sleek, sexy legs had made him fairly mad with longing. And when he'd whisked his fingers across her damp panties and connected with her moist private parts, he thought he'd been given a gift from the gods. Hell, he must have done something right in a past lifetime.

Just thinking about her triggered a reaction from his body. Perspiration broke out on his skin and clung to his upper lip. He instantly grew needy for her as he replayed the passionate slide show in his mind's eye.

Shit, he'd better tamp down his desires and censor his thoughts. This was not the time or place for such delicious memories.

As everyone at the table concentrated on the lovely meal before them, Kale redirected his focus. He wondered what Erin was doing at that exact moment. Would she be having dinner with her family? Hanging out with her friends or testing her bad-girl act with another man? A sudden surge of jealousy rushed through his veins and fired his blood. The flash of possessiveness made his stomach twist. He frowned and worked to dispel the image of Erin playing bad girl, or playing anything with another man.

Kale knew Erin was not simply a passing interest. She made him feel the way no other woman had ever made him feel. He liked everything about her, right down to her cute ponytail and dark, soulful eyes. There was no question about it. He wanted her, and not just on a sexual level. Kale had never been exclusive before, but he wanted exclusivity with Erin.

For a reason that he resolved to get to the bottom of, Erin was anxious to take a stab at being the bad girl she pretended to be. Fortunately, that gave him the perfect opportunity to take their relationship to the next level of intimacy and show her that he could be more than a casual sex toy. Not that he wasn't interested in being her sex toy, mind you.

A small grin tugged at his mouth as he conjured up the numerous ways to help her play the bad-girl act. Oh yeah, things around the lab were going to get very interesting. Because he planned on heating things up.

First thing tomorrow morning.

Starting in the elevator.

Night had closed around them as Erin sat at her mother and father's dining room table with the rest of her family. Her younger *married* sister, Terry, as her mother so frequently pointed out, and Terry's husband, Kenneth, fussed with their three-year-old daughter, Sarah. Her other sister, Kayla, the youngest of the three girls, hadn't been able to make it to dinner. Her husband was on call at the hospital, and Kayla had been up all night nursing her new newborn.

Erin swallowed her last bite of mashed potatoes and secretly thanked the Lord that she'd made it through another Sunday dinner without her mother bringing up her single status. It was rather refreshing to eat a meal in peace without visualizing herself stabbing something, or someone, with her fork. Thank God her father didn't pressure her too.

She caught her mother's glance. Oh no. Perhaps she'd jumped the gun. A familiar matchmaking gleam danced in her dark eyes and sent alarm bells skittering down Erin's spine.

The sound of Luke, her one-year-old nephew, waking from his nap in the other room gave her reprieve. His high-pitched cries were like music to Erin's ears.

Erin wiped her mouth and tossed her napkin onto the table. "I'll get him."

Excusing herself, she rushed across her mother's Persian rug, stepped into the living room, and walked over to the marble fireplace to scoop Luke out of his toy-filled playpen. "Hey Luke," she cooed, brushing his damp hair from his forehead.

As she snuggled his squirming body against her chest and inhaled his wonderful baby scent, her heart lodged somewhere in her throat. She fought down the unwelcome tug of emotions and set the rambunctious one-year-old down. The sound of dishes clanking in the other room, combined with the delicious aroma of apple pie coming from the oven, obviously held more appeal then being cuddled by his aunt. With supersonic speed, he disappeared into the kitchen. Erin grinned. The kid knew only one gear. Full throttle.

Before Erin could say her good-byes to her family and escape back to her condo to prepare her notes for tomorrow morning's experiment, her mother rounded the corner. Smoothing her short blond hair behind her ears, Anna lowered herself into her favorite French Provincial wingback chair, and neatly crossed her legs at the ankles.

Without preamble, her mother jumped right to the point. "I went Christmas shopping today, Erin."

Erin drew in air, and then plunked herself onto the matching sofa. Her stomach plummeted. She knew exactly where this conversation was headed. The same place it headed every time the family got together. She pressed her body deeper into the cushions, hoping the sofa would open up and swallow her whole.

She rubbed her temple, attempting to ward off an impending headache. "That's nice, Mom."

Anna's dark eyes widened in delight as she leaned forward in her seat. "Guess who I met at the mall."

"Santa?"

Pursing her lips, clearly disappointed in Erin's smart-assed comment, her mother continued, "Richard Wallis."

Erin groaned. Cripes. The sight of him taped to the flag-pole in high school with nothing on but his undershorts still plagued her memories.

"He's still single, you know."

Erin arched a brow. "Really, what a shocker. I would have thought women would be tripping over themselves to sink their claws into a thirty-year-old guy who sells watches out of his trunk and still lives with his mother."

Damn, Anna was really scraping the bottom of the barrel this time. The poor woman was getting desperate to marry off her ancient, twenty-eight-year-old spinster daughter. She'd obviously given up hope Erin would snag herself a rich doctor, like her youngest sister had. Now it looked as if anything with a penis would do.

Erin resisted the urge to roll her eyes heavenward. Like it was a freaking crime not to be married with kids by your thirtieth birthday.

Likely her mother had grown tired of fielding questions from the old windbags at her country club as to why her eldest daughter had yet to get married. It was simply scandalous.

Maybe Erin should just tell her mother she was a lesbian. That would really shake up the nosy old bats on card night.

Couldn't her mother understand that she had her career, which was all she needed? And couldn't she just be proud of Erin for working hard and earning the lead position for the latest project? And if this project turned out to be a success, she'd become head of her wing. Erin really didn't need anything more than that.

Which left her wondering why her heart turned over every time she held her sweet little nephew in her arms.

"He no longer does that, Erin. Richard now sells video games at the mall, and he makes a pretty decent living. I hear he holds some King Kong record."

Erin cringed inwardly. "It's Donkey Kong," she corrected. "I played it when I was a teen."

How freaking delightful. Her mother was setting her up with a guy who still played kid games. The last thing she needed in her life was another man who never grew up and took responsibility.

Erin's mother gave her a cool look and continued, "I bumped into him on the elevator."

Meet me in an elevator sometime.

Kale's parting words immediately rushed to the forefront and echoed in her head. Oh hell!

Despite the chill in her mother's voice, her body warmed all over. The reception had ended more than twenty-four hours ago, yet those words still played havoc with her body. She'd been unable to dispel the image of how delightfully naughty it would be to *bump* Kale in an elevator sometime. Lord, obviously it had been far too long since she'd answered the demands of her lascivious libido.

Kale, however, who had eagerly pointed out he was into casual sex, probably answered the demands of his body, one part in particular, on a nightly basis. Probably with a hot-looking Barbie-doll type too. Erin had never felt inadequate in the looks department, but she was no Barbie doll. Her boobs were *not* bigger than her brains.

The sound of her mother's voice jostled her back to the present. "Erin, are you listening to me?" Disgruntled, Anna furrowed her brow.

Erin drew in air. How was it possible that her mother could reduce her to feeling like a teenager with just one stern look?

"I am now," Erin offered brightly, struggling to marshal her inappropriate thoughts.

"Good, because we're having a Christmas gathering to-morrow night and Richard is coming here with his family. It wouldn't hurt for you to be nice to him."

Hurt? Oh no, it wouldn't hurt at all. And neither would electric shock therapy.

"And please try to do something with your hair."

Erin tugged on her ponytail. *Kale liked her hair.* Good Lord, she couldn't believe how many times that man popped into her head. She'd never lusted after anyone like this before. Not even her ex-fiancé. Maybe she was just going to have to have casual sex with him. Obviously, this celibacy thing had gone on long enough. It was beginning to interfere with her thought processes. And that just wouldn't do.

How was that for rational thinking?

"What's wrong with my hair?"

"You'd look a lot prettier and attract a lot more men if you did something with it."

Erin could feel the anger rising in her. "What if I don't want to attract more men?"

Her mother waved a dismissive hand. "Don't be silly, Erin. Of course you do."

Erin opened her mouth to protest. "I—"

Cutting her off, her mother continued. "I'll make you an appointment at Claire's for your lunch hour tomorrow. It's conveniently located just around the corner from your office. Be there."

With that nonnegotiable piece of advice, her mother stood and rounded the corner, disappearing from Erin's line of vision. Erin threw her head back and pinched her eyes shut. What would it take to get her mother off her back? Of course, Erin already knew the answer to that. A man. Apparently any man.

Erin could only imagine the look on her mother's face if she brought home a handsome, successful, confident guy like Kale. She'd probably have a coronary. Not that a playboy like Kale would be interested in coming home with her, mind you. Nor was she interested in bringing him home.

That would be much too personal.

So why the hell had she even thought about it?

Chapter 4

As Erin pulled her car into her assigned parking spot at Iowa Research Center, she unsuccessfully tried to block her mind to a riot of emotions rushing through her. Just knowing that she'd be working closely with Kale for the next month brought on waves of nervous anticipation.

Tightening her coat around her body to ward off the winter wind, she slid from the driver's seat and hustled across the parking lot.

A movement out of the corner of her eye caught her attention. Well, well, if it wasn't her nemesis, Hooker Barbie, or rather, Deanne Sinclair. A woman who was hell-bent on sabotaging Erin's career to claim what she believed was her rightful position as the lead scientist for the Pleasure Prolonged experiment.

Deanne stepped in front of her, blocking her path, forcing Erin to acknowledge her presence. Erin had never played with Barbie dolls as a child and she certainly had no intention of playing with one now.

Forgoing pleasantries, Erin muttered, "Excuse me," through clenched teeth as she tried to neatly sidestep her.

Deanne blocked her path, brushed her bleached blond hair from her face, and pasted on a plastic smile that was as fake as the conniving woman herself.

"Did you have a nice weekend?" Deanne asked, dark lashes blinking over fiery green eyes as her gaze raked over Erin's body, as though assessing the competition. "You sure seemed to have a nice time at the wedding."

Cripes, if looks could kill, Erin's loved ones would be pulling out their funeral attire. The woman really had it out for her since Erin had landed the coveted position. And now that she'd also landed the very sexy, very slurpalicious, and much coveted partner, Kale Alexander, she'd managed to stoke the embers of jealousy brewing below Deanne's cool, superficial surface.

"I had a terrific weekend," Erin said breezily, sailing past her. She gritted her teeth and picked up the pace. This was not the time to get into a pissing contest with Deanne. After changing her clothes for the hundredth time that morning, which had absolutely nothing to do with working closely with Kale, she had repeatedly assured herself, she was running a bit behind.

Shadowing Erin, Deanne hurried her steps to keep up. The sudden throbbing in Erin's head began beating a steady rhythm with Deanne's spiked heals.

"I know how important this position is to your career, Erin," Deanne said in a clipped tone, ignoring the fact that Erin had no desire to pursue a conversation.

Ice dripped from Deanne's voice and seeped under Erin's skin. Brrr ... Erin hugged herself to stave off a shiver. Had the temperature around her just dropped a few degrees?

"And I wouldn't want you to do something foolish to mess it up," Deanne continued.

Yeah, right. Everything in her calculating voice clearly indicated that she prayed Erin had a category five screw-up. She suddenly wondered if that huge load of crap spilling from Deanne's lips left a bad taste in her mouth.

Okay, so maybe she did have an extra minute or so for a pissing contest. And yeah, maybe all the clothes she had tried on earlier that morning had something to do with Kale. So what!

Drawing a fueling breath, Erin stopped mid-stride, twisted around, and questioned in a deceptively mild tone, "Something foolish?"

Deanne came up short and nearly crashed into her. The fake, high-pitched chuckle coming from Deanne's throat was more irritating than the sound of her neighbor's tweaked-out import peeling out of the parking lot at the most ungodly hours. It curdled Erin's blood and raised her pressure from simmer to inferno. As Erin conjured the ways she could put a stop to her neighbor's antics, her gaze drifted to Barbie's ample cleavage. She wondered what would happen if she let the air out of those imported inflatables. Would it shut Deanne down too?

Pleasure Prolonged

Erin slung her briefcase strap over her shoulder and stuck her hands in her coat pockets in an effort to resist the urge to inflict bodily pain on the other woman. She schooled her features into polite interest. "And what exactly is it that you think I would *do* that was foolish?"

Even though Deanne pouted her full lips and batted her long, thick lashes innocently, she still couldn't mask the look of disdain. Erin knew the woman had an agenda of her own. She made a mental note to be careful.

"Why Kale, of course," Deanne said matter-of-factly. "You two seemed pretty cozy at the wedding reception."

Erin wet her lips as the scandalous image of her *doing* Kale rushed through her mind.

Deanne's eyes gleamed dangerously. "I'm sure I don't have to remind you that the director frowns on such behavior. Stepping out of line at the center, or breaking protocol, could cost you your job."

Well, well, a Barbie with a brain. What an unusual, if not dangerous, combination.

Deanne cocked her head as she offered Erin a saccharine smile bright enough to light up the entire research center during a blackout. "You know how I'd hate to see that happen."

Yeah, about as much as Erin hated to see Barbie pinned under the wheel of her sporty pink camper. Just like the one Erin had purchased last week for her niece's Christmas present. The visual made her grin.

Deanne pursed her mouth, linked her fingers together, and gave Erin a once-over. "Then again, it's probably not something you have to worry about. It's not like a playboy like Kale would want anything from you. I'm sure it was a chore for him to slip that garter over your leg."

"Yes, and I'm sure it was a chore for him to kiss me with such heated passion when he discovered the mistletoe over our heads as well."

Deanne's face turned an odd shade of red, like a cross between a beet and a baked ham. She gasped in outrage. Her saccharine-sweet smile slipped from her face.

Pissing match over. Final score, one to nothing for Erin.

Deanne began mumbling something about the bouquet, an unfair toss, Kale, and mistletoe, but Erin tuned her out and let her gaze drift to the candy-apple red truck that had materialized in the lower lot. Maybe it would run Barbie down and put her out of her misery. No, put them both out of their misery, she corrected herself. Although Erin suspected that Barbie's plastic limbs would simply snap back into place.

The sound of Deanne's voice pulled her back. "This isn't over, Erin."

Using her tongue, Erin made a slow pass over her bottom lip, adding fuel to Deanne's slow-burning fire. "It's been nice chatting with you, Deanne, but I have to run. Kale's probably anxiously waiting for me."

Deanne snarled. "I'll be watching you."

Erin arched one brow and gifted her with an amused look, the juvenile side of her enjoying their push and pull far too much. "Really? Well, I'll try to make that as pleasurable for you as possible."

Shelving their conversation in the recesses of her mind, Erin turned her back to Deanne and rushed inside the lab's main building. She pushed open the heavy glass doors and stepped into the lobby. The warm air chased the chill from her body as she moved farther into the building.

Ribbons of sunlight followed her inside and gleamed on the cracked but freshly polished tiled floor. The building might have been old and run-down, but the janitorial staff kept it impeccably clean. The familiar, almost comforting scent of pine floor cleaner reached her nostrils as she greeted the front security clerk with a cheery Monday morning smile and flashed her identification card.

"Good morning, Mikey. How was your weekend?"

Michael's green eyes brightened as she stepped up to the counter. He sat up straighter in his seat as Erin leaned forward and signed herself in.

"Hey, Erin. Good morning to you too. You're looking beautiful as always."

Erin grinned and playfully batted her lashes. "Mikey, you say that every morning."

"That's because you look beautiful every morning." One dark brow lifted suggestively. "So what do you say, Erin. Will you go out with me this weekend?"

She dipped her head and chuckled, enjoying their usual innocent flirtation and easy banter. "Are you bringing your wife?" she teased, the same way she teased every other morning. Erin knew Mikey loved his wife more than life itself.

He pressed his hand to his chest. "Erin, you're breaking my heart."

She grinned and twisted on the ball of her foot. "Have a good one, Mikey." As she crossed the wide expanse of marble floor, she eyed the stainless steel doors of the elevator.

Meet me in an elevator sometime.

Her footsteps stilled as a fine tingle stirred her most erogenous zone. Good Lord, she needed to pull herself together. She diligently tried to shrug off his sexual invitation as she resumed her pace. Not only was it frowned upon to intimately consort with a colleague, as Deanne had so graciously pointed out, but she would never be able to get any work done as long as she continued to imagine the kinds of private, intimate things he would do behind the closed doors of an elevator.

Private, intimate things he would do to her.

She blew out a shuddery breath and surveyed the lobby. Deanne hurried past her and made her way to the stairwell. God forbid the woman took the elevator and stored a calorie. Of course, the fact that the antique elevator wheezed like a pneumonia patient and made unscheduled stops between floors, leaving its occupants trapped while it recaptured steam, made for another good reason to take the stairs.

Erin glanced around again. No sign of Kale. She released a sigh and ignored the odd wave of disappointment that stirred her blood. Cripes, she wasn't really considering having sex in an elevator with Kale, was she?

When the steel doors opened, she rushed ahead and stepped inside. Catching sight of her reflection in the floor-to-ceiling mirror, she smoothed her hands over her wind-blown hair.

Okay, okay, so she couldn't deny that she'd taken extra care with her appearance that morning as she carefully knotted her hair in a ponytail at the nape of her neck.

The way Kale liked it.

She touched her finger to her lips, and for the umpteenth time since the wedding reception, she relived Kale's sensuous kiss. Here it was days later, and that kiss was still messing with her mind. No man had ever kissed her like that before.

The truth was, the two men she'd been intimate with had spent more time worrying about their pleasure than hers. Her trips between the sheets were over long before they had even begun, leaving Erin having to take matters into her own hands.

Of course, there was that one time that she thought she'd had an orgasm with her ex-fiancé, but then she quickly realized the flutters in her body were from a bout of indigestion. That's what she got for eating pepperoni pizza before bed.

Something told her Kale would never leave her unsatisfied and frustrated. Her body fairly vibrated just thinking about how he'd undoubtedly take matters into *his* hands.

She drew her lip between her teeth and allowed herself another moment to reminisce about Kale's warm mouth over hers. To think he'd barely gotten started. She could only imagine how wonderful it would have been if he'd had the time to thoroughly explore her mouth ... her body. Damn, she could feel herself coming unglued just thinking about it.

She'd spent all of last night agonizing over how to proceed where Kale was involved. There was no denying the physical attraction between them. It was an attraction unlike anything she'd ever felt before. It set her loins on fire and muddled her usually clear thoughts. Kale had certainly made his intentions clear at the reception. All she had to do was gather her courage and play the part of the bad girl.

The woman in her told her to go for it. Have casual sex, enjoy it, and move on. Thanks to her ex-fiancé, she no longer believed in happily-ever-after and wasn't looking for a relationship.

Kale would be returning to Los Angeles in a little over a month's time and had made it clear he wanted her only sexually. They had no future. Nor did she want one.

On the other hand, the emotional part of her advised her to be careful, warning her that having sex with him would be a bad idea. Since her breakup with Dwayne she'd taken control of her life, her work, and her emotions. But when she was with Kale, that control seemed to pack up and leave town. The man threatened all her barriers. She wasn't so certain she could satisfy her sexual desires without the risk of feeling some deeper emotional connection with him.

Erin pressed floor fourteen on the glowing orange number panel and leaned against the wall. Her thoughts drifted. *Fourteen floors of wild, hot, untamed sex.* Whew. Time to shed her winter coat.

Moments before the doors pinged shut a pair of well-worn sneakers jammed between them, shaking the old elevator and bouncing the doors back open. Those sneakers led to a pair of faded jeans slung low on the hips. The jeans led to a very familiar tight waist, thick chest, and broad shoulders. Erin gulped.

Oh God, it couldn't be.

Her eyes locked with his.

Kale!

Oh God, it was.

Awareness flared through her as he stepped inside. His presence swallowed up the small space.

Desire flickered across his face as his gaze fixed on her with intent. His bad-boy grin curled her toes.

"Going down?"

She didn't miss the double entendre. His words sent a tingle along her nerve endings, sparking a pool of moisture to dampen the silky curls at the apex between her legs.

She took a moment to consider her situation. Here she was alone in an elevator with a gorgeous guy who oozed sexuality and sent waves of passion ripping through her. A guy who'd made it perfectly clear that he liked getting intimate in public places. A guy who wasn't looking for more than she could give. Her pulse kicked up a notch. A guy who didn't know she was all talk and no action. She had two choices, really. One, she could slip from the elevator and bolt, or two, she could slip out of her panties and put her money where her mouth was. Her gaze drifted downward to examine the massive bulge in his jeans. Or rather, his cock where her mouth was.

When she looked at it that way, it really narrowed down her choices.

He ran his fingers through his hair, his jaw flexed. He edged toward her. "Well?" he asked in a gentle yet commanding voice. She felt the rush of his warm breath over her cheeks and shivered in delight.

Perhaps she should have casual sex with him. That might help get him out of her system and put her focus back on her career where it belonged, especially if she wanted a shot at advancement. Surely if she tried hard enough she could engage in a frivolous affair and keep her heart out of the arrangement.

She nodded, not trusting herself to speak. Oh yeah, she was going down all right. Faster than a hockey player without his protective cup.

Lust. Need. And something else. Something intense and urgent whipped through Kale's blood as he leaned against the mirrored wall and perused the exquisite woman before him.

With her hair tied back, she was dressed in a dark turtleneck sweater that framed her flawless skin and heart-shaped face. A black, knee-length skirt flared around her legs. Her winter coat was draped over her arm. He was absolutely floored by her beauty.

His hungry eyes moved over her lush mouth, sexy curves, and shapely legs. He wondered if she wore thigh-high stockings or pantyhose beneath that silky skirt. He scrubbed his hand over his jaw as his fingers itched with the desire to discover all her sexy little secrets.

Pleasure Prolonged

He crossed one leg over the other and drove his fists deep into his pockets. As he watched her, heat gravitated south, his thickening cock indicating his needs and desires. He'd made it clear to her at the reception how much he wanted her. Now he was waiting for her to come to him. It was time to let her step into the role she so desperately wanted to experiment with. And when she did, she would see that there was a greater force at work here. This wasn't just about physical desire.

Still somewhat guarded, Erin took a small, tentative step toward him and opened her mouth to speak. He focused his attention back on her plump lips. Before she had a chance to talk, someone entering the lobby yelled for them to hold the doors.

Kale shifted his stance and poised his hand inches from the glowing "open doors" button. His eyes locked with Erin's, waiting for her to make the next move.

"What do you think, Erin, should we hold the elevator?" he asked, leaving the ball in her court, giving her the opportunity to play out her part and call the shots.

Something in her expression changed. Her face tightened warily. Her voice wobbled. "What if we get caught?" She tensed and eased backward.

He leaned forward and propped his hand on the mirror behind her, caging her in. "What if we don't?"

Her dark eyes were full of want as she mulled that over for a second.

He knew she wanted this. Hell, he did too. So much that he felt dizzy. But he also understood her reluctance to get intimate at her workplace. They both had their careers to consider.

"No one will see us, Erin," he assured her. "With Christmas only five days away, most of the staff has already left for their holidays. We practically have the whole building to ourselves." He tossed her a wicked grin as his gaze raked over her body. When he reached out and brushed his thumb over her mouth, he watched her unease segue to desire.

Mouth parted slightly, she drew a shaky breath and nodded toward the "close doors" button. Her beautiful brown eyes turned one shade darker as her sensuous lips thinned provocatively.

He had no idea he'd been holding his breath until he let out a rush of air. Kale stepped back, jabbed the "close doors" button, and then let his hand drop to his side. A thrill coiled through him as the heavy steel doors slammed shut, leaving them all alone in the slow, antiquated, dimly lit elevator.

As the elevator began an unhurried ascent, she dropped her coat onto the floor and moved toward him. He didn't want to wait another second to hold her in his arms. With a predatory advance, he was on her in seconds. His hands touched her all over, stroking, caressing, pulling and pushing, yet he still couldn't get enough.

She felt so damn incredible in his arms. Like it was where she was always meant to be. Her scent closed over him like heavy fog on a rainy day. His blood pressure soared as his heart beat in a mad rush. Fuck, he wanted her so bad, his body shook. He was shocked by the intensity of his need for her.

Her breathless voice washed across his face as she spoke. "I thought you could show me."

Sweet Jesus, please let them be on the same wavelength here. His heart thudded with hope. "Show you what?" he asked, brushing his thumb over her pink cheek.

Her long lashes flickered. Turbulent emotions brewed in the depths of her eyes. She thrust her pelvis forward, urging him on. "Show me the kinds of casual things you do behind the closed doors of an elevator."

He groaned and drew her tighter into the circle of his arms, his hands splaying over the small of her back. *Casual.* There was that word again.

Even though they'd known each other for only a short while, Kale knew there was more than *casual* between them. And he had fourteen floors to show her. He stole a glance at the number pad. Make that thirteen.

Thirteen floors.

Although it was not nearly enough time to kiss her, touch her, and leave her wanting more, he'd have to make do.

His fingers tangled through her hair as he angled his head closer. Yanking gently, he forced her chin up and her mouth open. She made a sexy noise, prompting him into action.

He cupped her face, surfed his tongue over her full, fleshy lips, and then drew them in for a more thorough exploration. Fuck, she tasted like she'd been coated in honey and dipped in sugar.

"Mmm . . ." he moaned and sucked harder, loving the way her mouth moved under his. Her deep purr vibrated through his body. Ah, now he knew. She purred.

The first touch of her mouth and ravenous swipe of her

tongue triggered an onslaught of emotions. As his chest tightened, it threw him off balance. Lord, he'd never dealt with these kinds of powerful feelings before.

Twelve floors.

Widening his stance, he captured her thigh between his and squeezed. His cock pulsed inside his tightening jeans. He sank deeper into her mouth and luxuriated in the enticing combination of flavored coffee and minty toothpaste. He felt her body liquefy against his.

"You taste so good, Erin."

"You too," she murmured between heated kisses, her eager hands coiling around his neck to pull him in tighter. She raked her fingers through his tousled hair and tugged. His heartbeat grew rapid.

Eleven floors.

"Kale?" she breathed into his mouth. Her heated breath scorched his flesh.

"Yeah?" He inched back to look into her dark eyes. Was she having second thoughts? His gut sank with the possibility.

Lust clouded her gaze. "You don't have to ask permission." Her voice thinned to a whisper, her face taking on a sexy, ruddy hue.

He tossed her a perplexed frown and brushed his thumb over her kiss-swollen lips. "Permission for what?"

She lowered her head, her lashes curtaining the emotions brewing in the depths of her expressive eyes. "Permission to touch me. Again. Down there." She pushed her pelvis against his thigh and gyrated. "Between my legs."

Sweet fuck. He'd seen the white tunnel and at the end was Erin.

Ten floors.

With renewed urgency, his lips came down harder, faster, taking full possession of her mouth. She matched the intensity of his kiss. His hand left her face and journeyed downward, reveling in the feel of her soft curves. He gripped both her delicate hands in one of his and secured them behind her back. Immobilizing her.

Nine floors.

She twisted and tensed. "What are you doing?" She sounded alarmed.

He knew she didn't like having her control stripped away, or feeling vulnerable, but he wanted her to let go and trust him. His voice was coaxing. "I want you to let go, Erin. Relax. Show me how much of a bad girl you really are," he said, urging her to give herself over to him completely.

Eight floors.

She opened her mouth to speak but no words formed as he delved beneath her skirt. He grazed her creamy thighs and was thrilled to discover she was wearing stockings. His fingers climbed higher until he touched her heated core. Dark lashes fluttered as she surrendered to his touch.

Seven floors.

She arched forward, her hips colliding with his throbbing erection. A gasp rolled out of her mouth when he gyrated against her. He groaned and clenched his jaw. Slipping his hand inside her panties, he used his fingers to make a slow pass over her channel, stoking her inner fire. He was damn pleased at how wet she was. Her throaty moan vibrated through his body.

"You're very wet, Erin."

Her head lolled to the side, and she rasped her next breath. "I know. You make me this way."

"Have you been hot and wet for me for days? The same way I've been hard for you all week?"

"God, yes," she cried out.

Six floors.

She spread her legs wider for him, inviting his touch. He dipped his finger deep inside her and growled as her tight sheath closed around him. Light ripples from the depths of her core began kneading his finger. He couldn't believe how close she was to coming.

"Did you spend last night thinking about having sex with me in this elevator? Did you think about all the naughty things I could do to you?"

She nodded, and he detected honesty in her eyes. That pleased him.

He put his mouth close to her ear. "Me too. All I could think about was touching you, tasting you, fucking you, and watching you come for me in this elevator."

As she moaned in response to his frank words, he felt her grow wetter.

Five floors.

A second finger joined the first. Kale closed his eyes as he took a moment to bask in her rich, decadent texture and luxuriously snug fit. He'd never felt anything better.

"You are so hot, Erin. And so responsive." He swirled his finger through her slick heat until his thumb found her clitoris. She worked her hands free and circled them around his back. Her nails clawed at his shirt as her body shuddered and jerked forward. "It's making me crazy."

"Kale . . . we need more time," she cried out.

Four floors.

He stroked her and teased her clitoris out from its fleshy hood. "We have all the time we need, for now," he whispered into her mouth before burying his lips against her throat. "Are you ready to come for me?"

She whimpered her response and pressed her hand over the bulge in his jeans and squeezed. His body reacted instinctively. "Fuck." He pushed against her and nearly came on the spot. He stroked her harder.

Three floors.

Gripping his shoulders, she ran her tongue across her lips and tipped her head until their gazes locked. She was panting. Her eyes were flashing, wild.

"*Please* . . . It's too much. It's too intense."

He could feel her orgasm pulling at her and knew it was time to take her over the edge. Using small, circular motions that drove her into a mad frenzy, he increased the pressure on her clitoris. He felt her skin grow tight with the first sweet clench of fulfillment.

Two floors.

Her breath came in a ragged burst. A flood of moisture erupted inside her. As her heat flowed into his hand, she clung to him and cried out his name. Her body trembled from head to toe. He held her tightly as she rode out the last waves of her orgasm. Watching her come made him wild with the need to fuck her. But that would have to wait. When he took Erin in his bed, it would be when they had all the time in the world. He wanted to lay her gorgeous body across his sheets and feast on her until they were both sated and exhausted.

"You're incredible, baby." He pulled his hand out from her panties and adjusted her skirt.

Her eyes were wide, glassy, unfocused. "Kale, I've never had . . ." Her words died away before she finished the sentence.

Fuck, was she about to say what he thought she was about to say? Was it possible she was trying to tell him that she'd never had an orgasm before?

Conflicting emotions passed through her eyes as she wet her bottom lip and continued. "I never had such a great time in an elevator before."

Kale wasn't about to push the subject. Soon enough he'd discover all her secrets. "The pleasure was all mine," he assured her and meant every word of it.

One floor.

The elevator light clicked off. Erin straightened and glanced at the bulge in his crotch. Her eyes went wide. "What about you? What about your pleasure?" Her chest heaved as she struggled to regulate her breathing.

Warmth encompassed him as his heart turned over in his

chest. She was so damn adorable. Her consideration of his needs and desires proved what he already knew. Unlike all the other women he'd dated, Erin Shay did not take without giving in return.

"Erin, it gives me pleasure just to watch you."

Her eyes opened wide, surprised. "Oh."

Kale pushed her bangs from her moist forehead and rained kisses over her cheek, her nose, and her jaw. Her soft skin felt like satin beneath his hungry mouth. He licked her earlobe, savoring the taste of her sweet flesh.

"I want more of you, Erin," he whispered into her ear. "I want to lick you and suck you and taste your sweet juices. I want you naked and writhing beneath me while I watch you come over and over again. Tonight. We'll finish this. Your place."

The doors began opening as they reached their destination. Erin pulled back, shook her head from side to side, smoothed her palms over her skirt, and stepped off the lift.

Kale's stomach took a nosedive as he watched her retreating back. He stepped from the elevator, grabbed her elbow, and turned her back around to face him. He slanted his head and met her glance. "No?"

Her eyes flashed with dark passion. "No, not my place, Kale." Standing on her tippy toes, she positioned her lips inches from his mouth. She ran her fingertips over his cheeks and smiled.

"Yours."

Chapter 5

Erin worked hard to keep her rubbery knees steady as she made her way down the narrow hall to the lab with Kale tight on her heels. Knowing she was going to have an encore performance tonight made her heart race and her mind whirl. Except tonight she was going to strip away Kale's clothes so she could touch and taste his gorgeous, athletic body. Her mouth began watering just imagining it now. She swallowed the saliva pooling on her tongue and tried to shake away the haze of arousal fogging her usually sharp mind.

She took a mental inventory of her wardrobe. Nothing quite seemed suitable for a night of hot, unadulterated, *casual* sex with a playboy who set her loins on fire.

She bit down on her bottom lip and gave further consideration to the situation. What on earth did one wear to such an event? Perhaps she'd skip out of work a bit early and stop by the mall and pick up a new dress. After that she'd grab a quick bite to eat and have a hot bubble bath before heading over to Laura and Jay's new house, Kale's home away from home during his month-long sabbatical. A mischievous grin curled her lips. Perhaps tonight she'd get a chance to try out the new hot tub Laura and Jay had installed before they left for their honeymoon.

She knew she had been quick to shut down Kale's suggestion to meet at her place. Since Dwayne, she had never invited a man into her territory. It was too personal. This was all about sex. Nothing more. She didn't want to risk the possibility that she might develop more than casual feelings for Kale. It would be much less complicated to go to his place and leave when the time came. No awkward sleepovers. No awkward good-byes.

This was just about the sex.

Nothing could ever come of it anyway. Besides the fact that Kale would be leaving in a month's time, neither of them wanted a relationship.

Kale was walking so close behind her, she could practically feel his warm breath on the back of her neck. His mere nearness turned her knees to pudding.

Cripes, she could hardly believe she just had sex in an elevator. Great sex! Fantastic sex! Actually, what she found even harder to believe was that she'd waited so long to have sex in an elevator. She should have tried this bad-girl act sooner.

Hell, if she had known how stimulating, how erotic it was, she would have been playing sex games every morning before work. Then again, she somehow doubted it would be that great with just anyone. Kale had a way of making her feel bold, and of unleashing her inner vixen.

Just knowing that the elevator doors could have opened at any second and she could have been caught with her pants down, or rather her skirt up, only added to the excitement, which really surprised her. She wasn't inclined to take risks with her career, but there was something undeniably enticing about Kale that had her acting completely out of character.

Suddenly, all kinds of other wicked fantasies that she'd suppressed began cropping up in her mind.

She slowed her footsteps as she approached the lab. Her liquid arousal made her panties damp and cold. She squeezed her thighs together and flinched. Kale gave her a curious glance.

"Everything okay down there," he whispered into her ear. The sexy rumble of his voice as it tumbled over her brought on a new wave of moisture.

Erin slipped her identification card into the electronic lock and punched in the code to her lab. "My panties are soaked. It's making me cold," she whispered even though they were the only two in the hallway.

At the sound of the buzzer, Kale pulled the door open and gestured for her to enter. "Take them off," he said as she breezed past him.

Erin stopped and turned back around. Cocking her head,

she lifted one brow and met his gaze. "And walk around all day without any panties on?" Now there was a suggestion she hadn't considered.

He stepped closer, crowding her. Something about the way his possessive gaze always settled on her mouth sent a delicious shiver pulsing through her body. Nobody had ever looked at her the way Kale was looking at her right now.

It thrilled her to know how much she enticed him. How much he wanted her. She hadn't felt this feminine and sexy in a long time. Deep down she secretly feared she no longer had any sex appeal because the last time she'd heard a whistle directed at her, she had to unplug her kettle. But her worries were unwarranted. The passion in Kale's eyes told her she had nothing to fear.

"Sure, why not?" His voice was husky, sensual, and fired her blood all over again. Her nipples swelled, crying out for attention.

She paused to consider his words. Why not? Honestly, she couldn't come up with one decent reason why she shouldn't peel off her panties. In fact, she could come up with a few good reasons why she should. Reasons like how it would affect Kale knowing she was walking around all day bare-bottomed under her skirt. Wasn't that exactly what a bad girl would do?

She pursed her lips and nodded. "Come to think of it, that's a great idea."

Boldly, she reached around Kale and pushed the lab door closed. After the latch clicked into place, she positioned her hands on her knees and slowly drew them higher, until she gripped the thin elastic bands on her lace panties. Her gaze never broke contact with his as she wiggled her hips and pulled the slip of material down her legs. She stepped out of them and twirled them around her finger, filling the air with her feminine scent. Kale's eyes darkened while his nostrils flared. She bunched her pink panties into a ball and stuffed them inside the front pocket of his jeans.

His eyes swept over her as his chest rose and fell with a deep intake of breath. "Jesus, Erin, I can't believe you just did that."

She grinned, a sexy, naughty grin that made Kale growl. This bad-girl act was turning out to be a hell of a lot of fun. She shrugged innocently. "Since it's entirely your fault that they're wet, you'll have to spend all day in here with me knowing I'm stark naked under my skirt." Giving in to impulse, she pressed her hard nipples into his chest.

Eyes smoldering with desire and heat, Kale gripped her curvy hips and pulled her against him, anchoring her to his body. His hands spanned her slim waist as his thick cock pressed against her stomach.

Oh my! She sucked in a breath as his impressive girth indented her flesh. She couldn't even begin to imagine how wonderful it would feel to have him fill her. To pump in and out of her with fervid passion. Or for her to climb on top of him and sink his magnificent length all the way up inside her while she rode him with wild abandon. Whoa. She really was turning into a wild, wanton woman.

He angled his head, and she knew he was going to kiss her. She parted her lips in silent invitation as her heart fluttered.

Her heart fluttered?

Oh God, she'd better watch it before she developed some deeper emotional connection with him. If she wasn't careful, she could easily lose herself in him. Heart and soul.

Since that wasn't an option, she steeled her emotions.

Before he had a chance to claim her mouth with his, the lab door swung open. Erin flinched and broke away from the circle of his arms.

None too gently, Kale grabbed her elbow and urged her back until her body collided with his. He pressed his lips close to her ear. His voice was dark, raspy, and richly seductive.

"Tonight, Erin. We'll finish this once and for all." The depth of emotion in his voice surprised her. Kale let go of her elbow and stepped back when Sam York, along with his chimpanzee, Rio, came sauntering into the lab.

Sam shoved his keycard back into his pocket. "Hey, thanks for holding the elevator, Erin," he blurted out, then paused when he spotted Kale. Sam's gaze darted between the two. "Oh, sorry, am I interrupting something here?"

Regaining her composure, Erin shook her head and tried for casual. "Not at all," she said, amazed to find her voice still functioning after that very intense moment. "Sam York, this is Kale Alexander. As you already heard, Kale will be doing research with me for the next month." Erin stepped close to Sam and nuzzled Rio's hairy neck. "And this lovely little girl is Rio." Rio flapped her lips and squirmed in Sam's arms.

Sam shifted his chimpanzee to his other hip and stretched his arm out. A grin curled his mouth. "So you're the lucky guy that gets to work with Erin. Did you lose a bet or something?" he teased.

Erin rolled her eyes at him and made a face. "And you're the lucky guy who doesn't," she shot back.

Not only was Sam a coworker, he was also one of her closest, dearest friends. He'd moved into the condo next to hers a few years previous and they had spent many weekends hanging out. Since Erin had grown up in a family of girls, Sam was like the big brother she never had.

Kale met Sam's outstretched arm. "Sorry about the elevator."

Sam furrowed his brow and glanced at Erin, regarding her for a long moment. She felt heat bloom high on her cheeks under his scrutinizing stare. She was sure he could see right through her. Sam knew her well enough to know the hue coloring her cheeks wasn't from the winter wind.

Sam's gaze dropped to Kale's front pocket. A thin piece of pink lace material stuck out for all to see. For all to know that she had ridden a hell of a lot more than just the elevator to the fourteenth floor.

Oh hell!

Kale must have sensed her unease. He angled his body sideways and quickly tucked it in.

She gave him a grateful smile and noted with dismay how that small, thoughtful gesture and the soft, intimate way he looked at her did weird things to her insides.

Sam cleared his throat and rolled his shoulders. "Yeah,

well, don't sweat it. Something tells me I was better off taking the stairs."

Like a child reaching for its mother, Rio stretched her arms out and leaned toward Erin. Erin hauled the chimp into her embrace, welcoming the distraction. She shot Sam a sidelong glance. "Don't you have somewhere to be?"

Sam raked his sun-kissed hair from his forehead and winked that sexy, familiar wink of his that had the women around the lab wiping saliva from the corners of their mouths. He hauled Rio back into his arms.

"You betcha. Your test subjects are here. I've already injected the male participant with serum, so if you and Kale want to step into the cage and get ready, I'll hook them up to the electrodes."

Erin dropped a kiss onto Rio's head before Sam headed out the door. She crooked her finger and nodded to Kale. "Follow me." She led him out into the hall.

"The cage?" he asked, moving in beside her.

She chuckled. "Sam's nickname for the control booth. It's no bigger than a birdcage." She opened the door and gestured for him to step inside. "Squeeze in." Her gaze leisurely traveled the length of his muscular body as he pushed through the door. Lord, he was big. Her glance fell to his backside, and she fought an urge to cop a feel. The man had an ass that erotic dreams were made of. She'd just bet she could bounce a quarter off those tight buns. "If you can manage to fit yourself in there," she added.

With his back pressed against the wall, Kale maneuvered

himself into the small room and grabbed a chair. Erin shuffled in beside him. With her professional demeanor back in place, she reached under the control console and flicked on a microphone button. A one-way glass mirror separated them from the naked couple snuggled under silk sheets in the adjoining research room.

She busied herself as she waited for Sam to hook the last electrode to the male test subject. Once the task was completed, Sam glanced up and gave a curt nod, signaling them to begin. Acknowledging him, Erin returned the nod.

After Sam left the room and secured the doors, Erin pressed "record" on the digital video recorder, enabling her to document the couple's activities and responses directly onto the computer database for future reference. She then clicked "play" on the DVD remote. The television in the far corner of the research room began playing an X-rated movie. The screen displayed a couple in a most erotic position. Sexy bedroom moans filtered in through the speaker.

Kale's eyes flew open. His jaw dropped. "You pipe in porn videos?"

Erin grinned. "You name it, we got it."

"Nice setup," Kale said, with a quick, appreciative shake of his head. "I should have crashed here instead of Jay's place."

"That's such a male thing to say." Erin rolled her eyes heavenward and flicked the light dimmer switch in the research room and in their booth, giving the subjects their privacy.

He cocked his head. "Well, I am a male, Erin."

She stole a quick glance at him. His sexy grin curled her

toes. Oh yeah, he was all male, all right. There was never any question about that. No one would dispute the fact that Kale Alexander was one hundred percent, prime-cut, grade-A, alpha male. The man should come with a government-inspected mark of approval stamped on his forehead.

Blocking her mind to the sudden surge in her hormones, she turned her attention to the monitors before her as they continued to record the couple's heart rate, blood pressure, and body temperature. Grabbing a pen and her notebook, she leaned forward in her chair and jotted down the current data.

Delicious moans and purrs curled around her, making her acutely aware of the virile male beside her. She was so conscious of his presence, his every movement, and his every warm breath. Suddenly his large body seemed to swallow up the already too small space. Heat flared through her as his heavy masculine scent saturated the booth.

So much for sex helping her focus her mind back on the job.

Seconds turned into agonizing minutes as they listened to the couple make love in the adjoining room. Growing restless, edgy, Erin shifted in her chair.

A sharp moan erupted from the female participant.

Kale cleared his throat and sidled closer. "What do you think he did to her to make her moan like that?" The deepening of his sexy tone hadn't gone unnoticed.

Unable to find her voice, she shrugged her response and mumbled something incoherent. Her mind began racing. She could think of a million things that Kale could do to make her moan like that. She licked her suddenly parched lips and swallowed. Lord, she felt like she'd eaten a bowl full of cotton balls for breakfast.

The speaker continued to feed in sounds of heated kisses and heavy breathing. The soft rustle of bodies moving on the silky sheets caused a fine tremor to move through her veins.

Damn. Was it getting hotter in the booth? Or was listening to the couple having sex toying with her libido? She took a deep breath in an effort to bank her desire; the effort proved futile.

"What do you think, Erin?" he prodded, his warm breath firing her senses. "What makes a woman moan like that?" The soft whisper of his voice was most seductive, creating an instant intimacy.

He edged impossibly closer, until his leg brushed against hers. His touch sent shivers skittering through her limbs. "What would make you moan like that?"

She suspected he already knew the answer to that question.

His smile was slow, predatory. "Never mind, don't tell me. I want to discover it on my own."

Her pulse leaped as her heart began to beat wildly. When she turned to look at him, she had to remind herself how to breathe. The intensity of the way he was staring at her robbed her of her very next breath.

Another moan from the research room drew her attention. She had difficulty taking her gaze off Kale. She had to force herself to concentrate on the control panel readouts.

She should be tracking the data, but Kale's leg rubbing against hers was too distracting. Too arousing. Her skin grew moist and tight as a maelstrom of sensations whipped through her blood.

He pitched his voice low. "I think he licked her."

Holy hell!

Her breathing grew shallow when he reached out and feathered the pad of his thumb across her lower lip, barely making contact. She almost drew the tip into her mouth for a long, thorough suck. Desire as she'd never experienced before gained her full concentration.

"Tonight when you come over, I'm going to lick you, Erin, to see if I can make you moan like that." His voice ended in a soft whisper.

Oh God! That got her attention.

Her body reacted to the lust she heard in his voice. She bit down on her bottom lip and anchored herself to her chair, resisting the urge to run to the rooftop to sing out in euphoria. She turned in her seat, and her eyes locked with his. He didn't have to *lick* her; his words were enough to elicit such a response.

She felt her nipples swell under his devouring gaze. Raw feminine need flowed through her. Her head began spinning as the room grew thick with the scent of her arousal.

He parted her lips with his thumb. "Only I'm going to make you moan louder." The wicked gleam in his eyes held all sorts of promises. Something in his expression told her he was more than capable of doing just that.

Cathryn Fox

The corners of his mouth lifted in a half smile as the fine lines around his eyes crinkled. Lord, he was so damn sexy when he turned on the charm and gifted her with one of his naughty playboy grins. A grin so full of sensual wickedness that any woman presented with it would pounce on him like he were a hot fudge sundae while she eagerly shed her panties.

The same way Erin had.

Out of nowhere, an odd surge of jealousy pushed back the lust and made her gut clench. What the hell was that? Cripes, it was disconcerting the way he aroused unwanted emotions in her. Erin took a moment to regroup and gave a silent prayer that her simple plan to play the part of the bad girl and indulge in casual, uncomplicated sex didn't come back to bite her in the ass.

Her attention glided over his face, then tracked lower to settle on his crotch. Once again lust clawed its way to the surface and overshadowed her battle with the green-eyed monster. Her breathing hitched and her eyes grew wide as she glimpsed his impressive arousal. Her responses to the sight of his erection seemed to please him.

Did the guy have any idea what his teasing was doing to her?

"In fact I'm going to make you scream," he said, his tone playful, yet so very, very confident.

When her gaze traveled back to his face, his trademark bad-boy grin widened.

Oh yeah! He knew exactly what he was doing. Well, two could play his game.

This time the male subject groaned. Erin placed her hand over Kale's leg. God, his thighs were so damn hard. The sudden image of her head nestled between them made her throat close over.

Trying for sultry, she leaned in and pitched her voice low. "What do you think, Kale? What did she do to make him groan like that?"

He gave a low growl of longing as sexual tension fired between them. His breath came in a ragged burst and tickled the sensitive flesh on her neck.

She slowly dragged her hand from his lap, linked her fingers together, and touched her tongue to her bottom lip. "I think she licked him." Her voice was a tight whisper. "Or maybe she drew him deep into her throat. What's your take, Kale?" Erin touched her fingertips to her neck and stroked up and down, mimicking what she'd like to do to him. "Do you think she drew him into her throat?"

Kale growled louder and shifted uncomfortably in his seat. His sounds of pleasure and need blended with the muted sex sounds coming from the corner speaker. The lust, agony, and sexual frustration swamping him were visible on his face. He opened his mouth to speak, but no sound formed.

Lord, by the look in his eyes, he was never going to make it until tonight. Erin knew that if Kale hadn't taken her edge off in the elevator, she'd have gone up in flames by now.

She inched her legs open, giving him an unobstructed view of her moist sex, driving him even wilder as she enjoyed for a moment having the upper hand. Erin had never reduced a man to putty before, and she had to admit, she quite enjoyed it. Frazzling a renowned playboy like Kale was such an empowering feeling.

Kale's gaze dropped to her arousal-drenched crevice. He scrubbed his hand over his chin and shook his head in agony. "Sweet fuck," he murmured.

Her heady female aroma mingled with his and reached Kale's nostrils. He drew a deep breath as his hands snaked out to cup the back of her neck.

The sight of her bare sex had washed the grin from his face. The change occurred so swiftly, it amazed her.

He cleared his throat and bent forward, his eyes dark and richly seductive. "You are such a bad girl, Erin, and so very naughty."

He tangled his hands through her hair and brought her lips close to his. She instinctively closed her hands over his arms and felt his corded muscles bunch. His eyes turned lustful, reflecting his every desire.

None too gently, he brushed aside a lock of her hair and pressed his lips possessively over her mouth. His tongue swept inside to mate with hers. His kiss was deep. Hard. Needy. Letting her know in no uncertain terms what the sight of her naked sex and the scent of her arousal had done to him.

He inched back. His voice was rough, barely audible. His eyes burned into her as they dimmed with desire. "Do you know what I do with naughty girls, Erin?"

She worked hard to recover her voice. "No, what?" She licked her dry lips and sat up straighter in her seat, eager to hear more.

Gaze riveted on her, he said, "I punish them."

Oh cripes! She gave a broken gasp and worked to get air back into her lungs. "Really? How?" she asked with heated anticipation. Damn, she should have at least tried to mask her enthusiasm a bit.

He gave a low growl of pleasure and spoke in whispered words. "Naughty girls need to be spanked, Erin."

Sweet mother of God!

If the predatory look in his eyes, combined with his devilish smile and his promising words, weren't a concoction for an orgasm, she didn't know what was.

Pleasure engulfed her as her nipples stood at attention. Oh God, she'd never been spanked before. How deliciously erotic. Lord, the man was relentless and knew how to push all her right buttons.

She bit her bottom lip before she did something telltale.

Like moan.

Chapter 6

The sound of the cage door rattling heralded someone's arrival and gained Kale's full attention. Without breaking the steamy hold he had on Erin, he inched away and starched his spine.

Director Reginald Smith stepped into the cage. As he pulled open the door, light from the hallway poured into the small, dimly lit booth. "Hey you two, how are things going in here?"

At the sound of their director's voice, Erin's face blanched, and her movements stilled.

Kale's head snapped up. He pushed back his rising lust, rested his elbow on the console, and with casual aplomb greeted the director. "Good morning, Reginald."

Reginald nodded his greeting as his eyes scanned the adjoining research room, surveying the experiment. "How are you two making out?"

"Quite well, as a matter of fact," Kale said, neglecting to tell him the exact details of how they were *making out*.

Keeping her back to the director, Erin exchanged a glance with Kale. A bevy of emotions passed over her eyes as she cleared her throat and worked to regain composure. It really pleased him the way he could get to her. Her guard was slipping, which meant things were getting personal for her, just the way he planned. A deep sense of satisfaction rolled over him.

Reginald leaned against the doorjamb. "Is everything on schedule?"

Kale looked pointedly at Erin, his heart tightening. Her bangs fell over her eyes, and he fought the sudden desire to brush them back.

"Everything is going according to schedule. Right, Erin?" Attempting discretion, he captured her ankles in his and eased her legs together. Blinking the lust from her eyes, she drew a steadying breath and gave him a grateful smile that warmed him from the inside out. She switched back to her workplace demeanor, clamped her thighs together, and swiveled in her chair to face the director.

She donned her professional face and smoothed her hair off her forehead. "Yes, everything is going according to plan." She spoke with a light tone, even though Kale knew it took effort. "We have test subjects lined up for every day this week, and then we'll compile the data and present our preliminary findings to you next Wednesday after the Christmas holidays."

Pleased with Erin's report, the director nodded, pushed off the door frame, and gripped the knob. "I'll look forward to that." He glanced at his watch and frowned. "I'm leaving shortly and won't be around for the rest of the week. Veronica and I are flying to Vegas." He rolled his eyes heavenward. "After Laura and Jay's wedding, she got it into her head that it was time for us to renew our vows."

Erin casually adjusted her skirt over her thighs, sat up straighter in her seat, and smiled. "That sounds like fun."

Kale narrowed his gaze, assessing the director. The expression on his face suggested that gouging his eye out with Erin's pen would be a whole hell of a lot more fun.

His brow furrowed. "*Fun* isn't the word I'd use, but at least I'll get to play the slot machines." He gave her a sly wink. "That was part of the agreement." He stole another quick look into the research room. "Looks like things are finishing up in there." He turned his attention back to Erin. "I'll leave an emergency contact with security for both of you."

He shot Kale a glance. "Try not to let her work you too hard, Kale. Erin has become quite the little workaholic. She'll keep you going all hours of the night if you let her."

He chuckled. "Erin has already been working me *hard*. But I don't mind one little bit." He angled his head. "I'm looking forward to observing all her extraordinary talents."

Erin's smile fell from her mouth as she turned back around to face him. He noted the way her body fairly shivered as she met and held his glance.

He arched a brow and leaned back in his chair, stretching his legs out until they collided with Erin's. "And I'm *up* for going all hours of the night. In fact, we are already planning on doing just that. Tonight. Aren't we, Erin?"

As she picked up the suggestive edge in his voice, her eyes opened wide. She made a face that suggested she was going to neuter him.

A little throttling he could handle. Hell, he might even like it. But neutering? No way, no how.

"I ... uh ... yes. Tonight. Working late," she mumbled, gripping her clipboard like it was a lifeline as she turned her attention to the data.

Reginald shook his head and shoved his hands into his pockets. "I guess I can't complain about dedicated employees. Keep up the good work, Erin. If all goes well with this experiment, you're guaranteed that promotion you've been after." He inhaled. "I smell much success in your future."

It occurred to Kale that Erin's drive and ambition matched his. The success of this project could take her from obscurity to making her mark in the scientific world. Kale remembered those days well and understood the importance of securing a career. He vowed to help her attain the future she so diligently strived for.

Reginald stepped out of the cage. Before he left, he turned back around. "Kale, can I see you in my office for a minute when you're done here?"

After the director disappeared, Erin threw her hands in the air. Her eyes flashed as she leveled him with a glare. "Are you crazy, saying something so suggestive like that in front of the director? Don't let his easy demeanor fool you, Kale. The man is sly. He knows everything that goes on around here."

God, she was so sexy when provoked. "Then I guess it's a good thing he's not going to be here for the rest of the week," Kale countered.

Just then Sam poked his head in the door. "Erin, they're finished. I'm unable to find Deanne to take care of the research room." He rolled his eyes. "Strange how she always disappears when there is menial work to be done. Would you mind getting a start on it while I do a quick coffee run?"

"No problem," Erin said.

Sam arched a brow. "The regular?" After Erin nodded, Sam turned his attention to Kale. "How about you, Kale? Are you a coffee drinker?"

"I'll have the same as Erin," he replied. "Black with one sugar. Thanks." When Erin lifted one perfect brow, he rolled a shoulder and offered no explanation for how he knew her tastes. The truth was, Kale knew a hell of a lot more about her than she realized.

"I'll be back shortly." With that, Sam pulled the door shut behind him, plunging them back into dimness.

Kale turned his attention to the research room. "Are they done already?" He squinted as his gaze panned the bed.

As Erin's eyes adjusted to the darkness, she squeezed her lids and glanced at the clock. "What do you mean, are they done already?"

Kale checked the time. "Erin, they were only in there for fifteen minutes tops."

"And you don't think that's enough time for multiple orgasms?"

The look he sent her pretty much summed up his thoughts on the subject. "It's hardly enough time to have multiple ..." He paused, searching for the right word. Shrugging, he added, "Anything."

She scoffed and blurted out, "I think fifteen minutes is ample time. That's ten minutes longer than what I'm accustomed to." Suddenly, as if realizing she'd given away too much personal information, she raised her hands and began backpedaling. "I mean ..."

He pressed his index fingers over her lips to silence her. His thumb brushed against her soft cheek. He could feel her skin grow warm under his touch. He loved it when she was so honest, so genuine, and gave him glimpses into the real Erin Shay. It made him want to take her in her arms and hold on to that part of her. Forever.

Back in the elevator, he had suspected no man had ever taken the time to give her the attention she deserved or pleasured her properly in the bedroom. Now this confirmed it.

Maybe it was an ego thing, but he had to admit, it pleased him immensely to know he'd be the first to take her to heights of passion she'd never known. And if he got his way, which he had every intention of getting, he'd be the first man, the last man, and the only man to give her multiple orgasms.

Cathryn Fox

"I'm going to rectify that, Erin. Tonight." His gaze drifted downward to leisurely inspect her gorgeous body. His cock pulsed, his hormones shifting into overdrive. He inhaled, filling his lungs with her scent. Christ, he couldn't believe how much he ached to lose himself in her heat. As his attention moved back to her face, he pulled her close and positioned his mouth over hers as he added, "All night long."

A sexy noise crawled out of her throat. A flurry of emotions passed through her eyes as she exhaled with extreme slowness. Her lids fluttered, and she seemed to be fighting the urge to close them.

The light in the adjoining research room flicked on, filling the cage with high noon brilliance, shocking them both back to reality. Kale eased away and jerked his thumb toward the mirror. "You go get started in there. I'll go see what the director wants, and then I have a mountain of paperwork to get through before tomorrow."

Erin stood and moved out of the cage. As she turned her back to him, he glanced at her lush ass, a sweet, voluptuous backside that he couldn't wait to cradle in his hands later that night. His tongue darted around a suddenly dry mouth as he conjured up the delectable image of her naked curves tucked neatly up against his groin.

Needing a moment to put himself back together before he met with the director, Kale made a quick trip to the washroom, splashed some cold water onto his face, smoothed his tousled hair back, and adjusted his jeans.

Feeling somewhat normal again, he moved down the hall

to the director's office. He was pleased that Reginald had summoned a meeting with him before he left for his Christmas holidays. Kale had planned on calling a meeting of his own to discuss the possibility of a transfer. Unfortunately, due to his current probationary status at Castech, he was certain there'd be far too many complications.

As he rounded the corner, he found Reginald's door ajar. Kale knocked and poked his head in. "You wanted to see me."

"Yes, Kale. Please come in." Reginald gestured with a wave. As Kale made his way across the room, Reginald swiveled on his chair and fished around inside his filing cabinet. "Here it is," he mumbled to himself. As he turned back around, his seat groaned like a wounded animal under his impressive weight.

Kale lowered himself into the plush chair facing the director's desk and observed his surroundings. Folding his ankles, he leaned back and made himself comfortable as he waited for Reginald to begin the meeting.

The director planted his elbows on his desk and without preamble got right to the point. "If this experiment goes as planned, Erin will be moving into a new position and we'll be looking to fill her old one. We could use a guy like you on our team, Kale."

Kale opened his mouth to voice his concerns regarding his probationary status, but before he could speak, Reginald cut him off and answered his unasked question.

He opened the file before him and spread his hands. "Even though you're currently on probation at Castech, I don't perceive that as a problem. I'll fight to get you on my team, Kale.

You're smart, you're a hard worker, Jay regards you highly, and your past accomplishments speak for themselves."

Kale took a moment to mull over the information. "So you're telling me if I accept the transfer, I'll be working under Erin." The sexy visual of him working *under* Erin made him hard.

Reginald nodded his head. "I realize that you've been the lead with your own team for many years and this position is beneath what you're used to, but it will only be temporary. If the production of Pleasure Prolonged goes as expected, and our funding comes through, next summer we'll begin trials on Pleasure Exchange, a female libido enhancer. By that time you'll be off probation and you and Erin will be given the lead."

Kale scrubbed his hand over his chin, pausing to consider the offer for a moment.

"I don't need an answer today, Kale. But please think about it, and we'll discuss the terms when I get back from Vegas."

Kale nodded his consent, even though he knew he had nothing to think over. He couldn't imagine finding a better place to work than under Erin.

Still shaken up and slightly chilled over the director's unexpected appearance during a very intimate moment between her and Kale, Erin grabbed her long white lab coat from her locker and shrugged it on. As she prepared to leave the lab to meet Sam in the research room, the shrill of the phone drew her attention.

Dropping onto the stool, she reached for it. "Hello."

"Erin, darling, I'm so glad I caught you."

Erin could feel her blood pressure rising, anticipating the conversation ahead. She gritted her teeth and tightened her coat around her waist. "Hello, Mother."

Forgoing pleasantries, her mother rushed on. "You didn't forget about your lunchtime hair appointment, did you?"

Erin's free hand automatically curled around her ponytail. "Of course not," she said, gripping the phone hard enough to turn her knuckles bone white. "Unfortunately, I can't make it. I'm swamped today and I'll have to work through my lunch hour."

Tense silence met her words and stretched on endlessly.

Erin waited for a long moment and then finally broke the uncomfortable quiet by asking, "Are you still there?" Lord knew she really didn't have time for this.

Her mother ignored her question and asked one of her own. "Shall I change the appointment until after work then?"

Erin pinched the bridge of her nose. "No, I have to work late tonight too."

Even though she was deep in conversation with her mother, she knew the exact moment when Kale had entered the lab. She was so in tune with him, she felt his presence and his heat long before she set eyes on him. She angled her head and watched him saunter across the floor to his desk. Just the mere sight of him sent her heart racing and pulse thudding. God, it was shocking what this man did to her.

When he arched a brow in a silent question, Erin held up her index finger, indicating she'd need a minute.

"How late?" her mother asked, clearly annoyed.

She turned her focus back on her mother. "Late enough that it doesn't look like I'll be able to make your Christmas gathering."

Silence reigned once again.

Deep down, Erin knew her mother had her best interests at heart. Anna's generation simply couldn't understand that the independent woman of today didn't need a man to make her happy. Still, Erin just wished her mother would respect her and stop trying to meddle in her affairs.

"But Erin, what about Richard? What will I tell him? He's expecting you to be here."

Noticing the curious look in Kale's eyes as he overheard the one-sided conversation, Erin knew this was not the time or place to be discussing her love life, or lack thereof, with her ever persistent mother. "I'll try to make it, okay?" she said, appeasing her for the time being.

"I'll see you at eight then, dear." Erin cringed at the self-satisfied musical note in her mother's voice. "You'll thank me, Erin. Just wait and see," Anna added.

Erin hung up the phone, glanced at Kale, and threw her arms up in the air. She blew out an exasperated breath and rolled her eyes heavenward. "Mothers."

Kale pushed away from his mountain of papers, and with two easy steps, moved into her personal space and furrowed his brow with real concern. He brushed a wayward hair from her cheek and tucked it behind her ear. Erin gulped air. God, when he looked at her with tenderness and touched her with such gentle hands, it made her forget he was a playboy, and she was playing the role of a bad girl.

She wanted to avert her gaze, but the look in his smoldering blue eyes held her captive and did strange things to her insides.

When he dipped his head her body went all tingly. His delectable scent curled around her as her flesh tightened in response to his nearness. "Is everything okay?" His voice was low, rough, and softly seductive.

When her eyes met his she felt a stirring deep in her soul. The attraction between them was the most powerful thing she'd ever felt. She dragged in a shuddery breath as the overwhelming need to touch him, to make a connection, consumed her.

"What is this gathering you can't make?" he probed.

She hadn't meant to get into her personal life, she really hadn't, but the warm timbre of his speech and the tenderness in his lilt melted her resolve and had her spewing like a leaky faucet.

"My mother is having a Christmas get-together tonight and she's setting me up on a date, which I don't want any part of. The woman is hell-bent on marrying me off. It doesn't matter how many times I tell her I'm not interested in a relationship, dating, or marriage; she continues to go behind my back and scheme."

Kale's warm, intimate smile liquefied her knees and tugged on her emotions. The logical part of her warned not to get too close, but when he looked at her as if there was more than *casual* between them, it awakened feelings she'd suppressed for years. Needing to put some distance between them, Erin took a measured step back and moved toward the lab door.

As Kale followed her into the hall, his fingers closed over hers, warm and strong. He squeezed, offering his comfort. As she absorbed his heat, Erin felt a churning in her gut and worked to ignore it.

He shook his head slowly as he moved in close. Walking by her side, he accompanied her to the research room. "I understand your dilemma completely, Erin. My mother has been looking for grandkids for years. I had dinner at her place last night, and she asked when I was going to find a woman to cook for me." He gave a quick shake of his head and chuckled.

Erin crinkled her nose and thought about her own exceptional culinary abilities. It occurred to her if his mother's only criterion for a daughter-in-law was cooking skills, Erin would be the perfect woman. She loved being in the kitchen. Cooking relaxed her. She'd even taken an evening course a few years back.

Not that a playboy like Kale would be interested in bringing home a closet domestic like her, mind you. Nor was she interested in going home with him.

That would be much too personal.

So why the hell had she even thought about it?

Erin tilted her head. "Are you and your parents close?"

He nodded. "It's just my mom and two sisters. My dad died when I was a teen."

She squeezed his hand in a silent message. "I'm sorry, Kale."

He smiled his appreciation. "We're all close. I took over dad's parental role and kept my sisters on a pretty tight leash. Lisa is just finishing up her last year at college, and Jenna will be starting next fall." He got quiet for a moment. "I miss them a lot," he added, almost to himself.

"Then why did you go out west? You could have worked here, at the research center."

"The pay was better at Castech. I needed the money to pay for their tuition."

Erin felt an odd tug on her heartstrings. Who knew Kale was so loyal, nurturing, and responsible where his family was concerned? "They must miss you terribly."

He nodded. "I think they do." He paused and grinned. "Every time I come home, Mom brings up grandkids. She's getting desperate."

Erin eased her hand out of his, reached into her lab coat, and pulled out her keycard. She slid it into the electronic lock. Kale pushed the door open and gestured for her to enter the research room.

Erin breezed past him and tossed her words over her shoulder. "At least your mother isn't trying to set you up with a thirty-year-old Donkey Kong champion who talks into your breasts and not your eyes."

"Um . . . well . . . I would hope not, Erin," he replied, securing the heavy door behind him. "Unlike yours, my breasts are pretty uninspiring." Humor edged his voice and played down her spine.

Realizing how ridiculous she sounded, she chuckled and turned back to face him, making light of the situation. "Unless of course you're into that kind of thing," she teased.

His glance flicked over her curves. "I think you know I'm not."

Oh yeah, she knew all too well.

"So why is she trying to set you up and marry you off?" he asked, his genuine concern evident in his expression.

She threw her hands up in the air. "Apparently it's a crime to be twenty-eight and single." Erin blew out a heavy breath and gave a tight shake of her head. "I have my job and that's all I need. I just wish she could accept that."

Moving across the wide expanse of tile, Erin sauntered over to the bed and pulled back the sheets. The sudden image of Dwayne the Dog screwing his slut secretary passed through her mind. Flustered, she mumbled under her breath, "No one seems to support my career."

His voice softened. "I'm sure she just has your best interests at heart."

Erin nodded in agreement. "I know you're right. Deep down she does, but regardless, it still irritates me."

"What time is this gathering?" Kale asked.

His question took her by surprise. Why would he care about that? "What?"

"What time is the gathering?" he repeated as he crossed to the other side of the mattress to help her remove the bedding.

She looked at him, really looked at him as he sauntered by her. God, he was so beautiful. His sexy, athletic gait turned her insides to mush. A rush of sexual hunger moved through her, swamping her with desire.

Realizing he was waiting for an answer while she took great pleasure in the sight of his gorgeous backside, Erin reached for the blankets and blurted out much too hastily, "Eight." She scooped up the linen, and with a quick twist, walked over to the hamper to dispose of the soiled bedding.

"I'll take you."

His whispery soft voice was excruciatingly gentle as it carried across the room and fell over her.

She spun around. "What?" she blurted a second time. She resisted the urge to slap her forehead. Cripes, she really needed to work on her verbal skills.

He shrugged easily. "Maybe if she sees you with me, she'll stop trying to set you up." The hoarseness in his voice felt like a rough caress, and it did torturous things to her body.

"If she sees me with a smart, successful, sexy guy like you, Kale"—her gaze panned his body as she spoke the truth—"she'll have a coronary."

Kale smiled at the endorsement. "Should we risk it?"

Erin tapped her chin, as though mulling over the idea. "Well . . ." she said.

Kale raised an inquisitive brow and advanced purposefully

as he circled the bed. He touched his finger to her chin and with the lightest caress, brushed it along her cheekbone.

"Well?" he asked. His deep voice flowed down her spine like warm honey and made her quake from the inside out. He lowered himself onto the unkempt bed, slipped his arm around her waist, and tugged her down beside him. "Do you want to get her off your back or not?"

At that moment, all she could think about was getting Kale onto his!

Sitting there, ensconced in the circle of his arms, she became conscious of the cushiony mattress below her, tempting her, filling her mind with wild and wicked ideas.

She linked her fingers together, resisting the urge to tear off his clothes and sample his fine body the same way he'd sampled hers in the elevator. Of course, this was not the time or place for such luxuries. That would come later. Tonight. At his place. She sucked in a tight breath and tamped down her carnal thoughts for the time being.

"I appreciate the offer, Kale, and as much as I'd like to see the look on her face if I paraded someone like you through her house, I'll pass. Besides, we already have plans for tonight."

At the mere mention of tonight, and the promise of erotic things to come, Kale's baby blues darkened with desire.

When she looked deep into his eyes, something warm, intimate, and potent passed between them, leaving her feeling breathless. She dragged in a huge breath, yet couldn't seem to fill her lungs.

He touched her cheek. "Erin ..." he whispered, letting

her know with just one word how much he wanted her. His sensual mouth parted as his glance locked with hers. He was going to kiss her, his intent clearly evident in his passion-imbued eyes.

Moistening her lips, Erin knew this was not the place for such intimacies. Her words of protest were lost on a moan when he leaned into her and captured her mouth with his. All coherent thought vanished, leaving her completely spellbound in the moment as his warm lips moved languidly over hers.

Blood raced through her veins as he took full possession of her mouth, drawing her in deeper for a mind-numbing kiss. He smothered her heated mewls of pleasure with a low growl of longing.

She began trembling from head to toe as he dragged her into his arms and eased her back onto the mattress. Using his weight, he pinned her under him. He angled his body over hers as their tongues touched and tangled.

Warmth pooled between her thighs as her sex muscles began thrumming. His hair tumbled forward and brushed against her cheeks in silken waves. Her whole body went up in flames as his hard muscles pressed against her soft curves.

He licked, kissed, and sucked like he couldn't get enough of her. She understood that feeling all too well. Her hands raked through his hair, gripping and pulling, unable to get her fill, unable to assuage the hunger tearing at her insides.

God, she'd never felt so needy, so out of control before. It occurred to her she was completely at his mercy.

Cathryn Fox

His voice sounded strangled, his breath coming in jagged bursts. "I want you so much, Erin, I ache." With fierce possessiveness his tongue delved deeper to explore her every crevice, her every secret.

When she glanced into his turbulent eyes, she was astonished by the raw emotions that tugged at her. Her stomach tightened, her heart fluttered. Some inner voice warned her that there was more than physical desire driving her actions and need for him. Self-preservation urged her to run. To run as far away from him as possible. But she knew she could no more move away from this man than she could move a mountain.

He rolled to his side, his large body pressing against hers. The raw, hungry look in his eyes sent a plethora of sensations rushing through her.

His corded muscles shifted as his hands skimmed her curves and dipped below her skirt. With the utmost expertise, he gently inched her knees apart.

"Oh God," she whispered, barely recognizing her voice.

He feathered his fingertips over her quivering flesh. "I want you, Erin. I want to be inside you. I want you writhing beneath me while I feel your hot juices drip over my cock when you come for me. But mostly I want to taste you."

Erin shivered almost violently as his darkly seductive timbre seeped under her skin.

Slowly, gently, his hands slid over her legs to her inner thighs. His fingers traveled higher and higher until he found her warm sex. He pulled open her dewy lips and idly stroked her aching clitoris. Erin gripped the mattress as her skin came alive. She began panting heavily.

His nostrils flared. "Tell me you want me." He breathed the words into her mouth.

The aroused edginess in his tone made her tremble. She worked to recover her voice, and shared in his urgency. Her hands raced over him. "I want you, Kale." Oh how she wanted him. She craved him with an intensity that was as arousing as it was scary.

His lips abandoned hers and moved to her neck. His mouth felt like fire on her naked flesh. Sounds of pure carnal delight erupted low in her throat. Blood pulsing hot, she melted underneath his touch as his warm, scented breath and heady male essence curled around her.

She wrapped her arms around his shoulders. "Oh God, Kale." She began moving, writhing, pressing against him like a wanton woman, her long nails biting into his flesh, leaving their mark as though she were branding him.

The logical side of her warned she was getting in way over her head, but the rest of her didn't care. The chemistry between them was explosive. She craved him with every fiber of her being.

The warmth of his skin seeped under her flesh as he positioned himself over her. Rational thought packed a bag and headed south for vacation, leaving her libido calling the shots. She moaned louder and moved restlessly below him.

Her responses to his touch seemed to please him. He growled and thumbed her engorged clitoris. "I love it when you move like that."

She arched her pelvis forward, driving his hand harder against her cleft. "Like this?" she asked, barely able to see straight in her current haze of arousal.

"Yes. Exactly like that." He rewarded her efforts by pushing a finger deep inside. His fingertip worked around her over-sensitive hot button that sent fire pitching through her blood.

Her whole body came unglued and quaked beneath his expert ministrations. "I'm . . ."

"I know, Erin. I can feel your muscles tightening." He lowered his voice to a mere whisper. "Close your eyes, babe. Don't think. Just feel. Open yourself up to me and concentrate only on the sensations," he commanded in a gentle voice.

She complied. Erin let her lids slip shut, bit down on her bottom lip, and focused on the sparks of pleasure igniting her loins.

Pleasure forked through her as he slipped another finger inside, filling her. He moved his two fingers in and out, changing the tempo and rhythm until he took her as high as the moon and stars. Shivers of warm need tingled through her body as he kept up the gentle assault.

Moaning, she fisted his hair and moved against him. She began trembling and panting as the rippling waves of her orgasm took hold. Her muscles clenched around his fingers as she gave herself over. An onslaught of pleasure made her cry out. Her erotic whimper filled the room as she rode out every delicious, pulsating, clenching fragment of release.

A moment later, as reality inched its way into her thoughts, she opened her eyes and looked at Kale. His warm, intimate smile turned her inside out.

"Hey," he said softly, brushing her damp hair from her forehead.

"Hey yourself." She drew a contented breath. "That was amazing." She blinked, working to refocus her eyes. Lord, that was two for two. The guy had great stats.

As if he read her thoughts, Kale cocked his head and said, "Two orgasms. And before lunch at that."

She gave a contented sigh. "Must be my lucky day."

Kale grinned wickedly as he trailed his fingers over her chin. "And to think the day isn't over yet, Erin." He sent her a look of intimacy and promise. Erin shivered.

She felt his cock press into her. She slid her hand between their bodies and cupped his arousal. She gave a soft moan of approval and whispered, "And it's going to be an even luckier night. For both of us."

Suddenly realizing exactly where she was, she tilted her head and looked past his shoulders into the control booth. Her stomach plummeted. Her mouth went desert dry. She turned back to Kale. The look in his blue eyes told her he'd read her unease and felt the tension rising in her.

"What is it?" Kale asked inching back.

"I don't know. I just got a strange intuitive feeling that someone was watching us."

Fuck!

Kale jumped to his feet and hauled Erin up along with him. His gaze darted to the control booth, but with the lights off in that room he couldn't see inside. As he turned back to Erin, he berated himself for acting like a hormonal teenager.

Nice move, dumbass!

Ravishing her in a viewing room at the center was one hell of a way to prove he cared about her and her career.

He worked to rein in his lust. "Sorry about that. I didn't mean to get so carried away." Christ, he really needed to learn to control his urges. He just couldn't seem to keep his hands off her. And honestly, he wanted so much more than to give her a quick, hurried orgasm. But the sudden need to hold her, to kiss her, and to possess her overshadowed rational thought.

He shoved his hands into his pockets where they couldn't get them into any more trouble, and mumbled curses under his breath. "You finish up here." He jerked his head toward the cage. "I'll go check it out."

Erin stole another glance at the booth. Kale followed her gaze. The light in the cage flicked on, allowing them to see inside. Erin let out a relieved breath when she spotted Sam moving around the cage, then mumbled something under her breath that sounded like "Hooker Barbie and pissing contest."

"Did you just say Hooker Barbie?"

Erin waved a dismissive hand and gave a tight shake of her head. "Never mind. Long story. Let's just be sure to keep our pleasure games in the bedroom." Then as an afterthought she leaned into him and added in a soft voice, "Or the elevator."

With that last thought in mind, Kale turned and made his way into the hall. "I'd better go dig into that paperwork. I don't want to be buried in research all night." He turned back to wink at her. "I have much better things to bury myself in."

Kale stepped into the hall and bumped into Sam coming from the cage. In one hand he held a tray with two cups of coffee, in the other he gripped a manila file.

Sam gestured with a nod toward the lab. "Your coffee is on your desk."

Concluding that Sam hadn't witnessed their indiscretions, Kale gave a curt nod. He twisted to leave, but Sam's words of warning stopped him mid-stride.

"I don't want to see her get hurt, Kale."

Kale turned back and met Sam's somber glance. It occurred to Kale that Sam cared a great deal for Erin and acted as her protector. Kale suddenly had a whole new respect for the man.

"I don't plan on hurting her," Kale assured him.

Sam widened his stance. "She's special to me. I don't know what this *thing* is going on between you two, but if you hurt her, I'll hurt you. Understand?"

Kale smiled and held his hand out for a shake. "Understood," he replied.

After a quick handshake to seal the deal, Kale said, "It's nice to know that you care about Erin and that you look out for her safety, but I'm going to take over that role from you now, okay?"

Sam narrowed his gaze, assessing him.

Kale drove his hands into his pockets and pitched his voice low. "I got it bad for her, Sam. And I plan on taking this *thing* between us the whole distance."

Sam's brow rose. An equal mixture of surprise and pleasure registered on his face. "Really?"

"Really," Kale said, meaning every word of it.

Sam gave a slow nod of approval. "It's just that she's been hurt in the past and I didn't want to see it happen again."

Kale addressed his worries. "I suspected that, and if I have anything to do with it, she won't ever get hurt again."

Sam clapped him on the shoulder. "Glad to hear it." Relaxing his posture, Sam gave Kale the once-over. "I really wasn't looking forward to taking you out back and kicking the shit out of you."

Kale chuckled, picturing the brawl going an entirely different way. "I wasn't looking forward to that either. And Sam, keep this conversation between us. Erin isn't ready to know how I feel yet."

Just then Deanne came sauntering down the hall. Sam turned his attention to her. "Deanne, I've been looking for you. I need you to retrieve the digital readouts from the recorder and log the responses."

"I'm on it," she cooed, slipping between the two, her body brushing provocatively up against Kale's in a very suggestive manner.

After she disappeared into the cage, Sam gave Kale a quick nod and gestured toward the lab. "Go drink your coffee while it's still hot. If you need any help with the paperwork, give me a shout." With that, he turned and made his way down the hall.

Kale hurried to the lab, planning to immerse himself in his work, hoping it would keep his mind off Erin and the things he was going to do to her lush, responsive body that night when she showed up on his doorstep.

Grabbing a seat at the desk, he raked his hands through his hair and perused the data. The feminine scent of Erin still clung to his skin. He inhaled, filling his lungs with her aroma as he recalled the warmth and texture of her body beneath his. When he slipped his finger inside her tight sheath and had found her so wet and willing, he'd nearly erupted on the spot. Christ, if he didn't soon take the edge off himself, he was never going to surpass her five-minute record.

Censoring his thoughts and turning his attention to the mountain of paperwork before him, Kale sipped his coffee and buried himself in his research. While he was lost in the data, time flew, and before he knew it, the day had passed him by.

Leaning back, he rolled his head to the side and took a quick glance out the lab window. The winter sun kissed the horizon as it began its nightly descent.

Both Erin and Sam had been in and out of the lab throughout the day as they continued their final testing on the serum and prepared a new batch for tomorrow's experiment, but Kale had barely lifted his head from his research, stopping only long enough to grab lunch.

A little over an hour ago, Erin had poked her head in to let him know she had errands to run so she'd be skipping out early, a rarity for her, he was certain.

As his mind wandered to the wonderful things he was going to do to Erin later the evening, a knock sounded on his lab door and drew his attention. Stretching, he climbed from his chair and sauntered across the room. He opened the security door and found an envelope. He tore it open and inside found a note that simply said, "Meet me in the research room."

He stepped into the hall and looked around briefly. When his search turned up empty, he moved toward the research room. Slipping his keycard into the lock, he pushed the door open.

He was immediately greeted with soft music and blackness. Taken aback, he groped for the light.

Before he could find it, he heard a shuffle a few feet away and a soft mewling sound. What the hell was going on? He hadn't expected this from Erin, especially after their risky indiscretions earlier that morning.

"Erin?" he asked, a little confused by her behavior.

"Shh ..." The smell of jasmine reached his nostrils. He inhaled the aroma and didn't link the scent with Erin. A movement against his body signaled his seducer had reached him. Silence fell over them like a thick blanket as small hands gripped his and led him across the room. He knew where he was headed. Straight for the cushiony bed.

Once they reached their destination, those same small

hands traveled over his body, going higher and higher until they snaked around his head like a scarf. His cock pulsed to life as she raced her fingers through his hair and dragged his mouth to hers. The minute their lips connected, Kale's stomach lurched. He knew the woman he held in his arms was not Erin.

He pulled back abruptly, breaking the contact. The small arms that were curled around his neck became unlinked and fell from his shoulders. A broken gasp filled the room. "Kale, wait."

He didn't immediately recognize the voice. Taking a distancing step, Kale reached for the lamp beside the bed and flicked it on.

He squinted as the bright beams reached his eyes. Blinking his gaze into focus, he glared at the woman standing before him. Jesus, he hadn't expected this.

"Deanne, what the hell are you doing?"

She stepped forward, crowding him. Inching herself onto her toes, she pressed her body against his and slowly, seductively twined her hands around his shoulders. "I thought we could finish what we started at the reception," she cooed, flashing him a bright, toothy smile.

Kale slid his hands up her arms until he found her fingers. He pulled them apart and pressed her arms into her sides. "I don't remember starting anything at the reception."

Ignoring the blatant coolness in his voice, she arched a brow. "Come on now, Kale. We both felt the chemistry between us when we shared a dance."

For a long moment he said nothing, just stared at her. The woman had *casual* written all over her, out to get what she wanted without regard for anyone else.

He gazed the length of her. Long blond hair cascaded over her delicate shoulders. Green eyes opened wide as she stared up at him with seductive prowess. She moistened her lips and arched forward, just enough to afford him a view of her ample cleavage. She was beautiful. Breathtaking, really. With a body that would rock any man's world. But he felt nothing. Absolutely nothing.

There was a time he'd have jumped at her offer. But that time was long gone.

He cocked his head, giving her a confused look. "I'm sorry, Deanne. I think you might have read me wrong." He backed up, but she only moved closer.

Her mouth turned down in a pout. She threw herself at him and clung to his shirt like lint. "I don't think so, Kale. You know there is more between us." Her lips closed over his and sent him stumbling backward, onto the mattress. It took great effort to peel all ninety-five pounds of her off him and stand.

After disentangling himself, he crossed the room and pulled open the lab door. Stepping into the hall, he reclaimed his personal space. "There is nothing between us," he bit out. "And there never will be."

Was it just his imagination, or did he see a wry smile curl her lips before he turned to leave?

Chapter 7

High overhead the crescent moon glistened in the dark sky as Erin made her way up the cobblestone walkway leading to Laura and Jay's two-story Victorian home. The brisk night air felt cool against her exposed legs, not to mention the other parts of her body she'd left bare. Her warm breath turned to fog as she exhaled. Lord, it was cold.

As she drew closer to the door, part of her couldn't believe she was doing this, yet another part of her couldn't wait to feel Kale's callused hands stroking her naked flesh, his sensuous lips moving over her mouth, her breasts, and other, more intimate parts of her body.

Shivering, which suddenly had nothing to do with the cold wind and more to do with knowing Kale was waiting for her, Erin tightened her coat around her waist and raised her hand to buzz the doorbell. Before she had the chance to press the button, the front door swung open.

"Oh." She stepped back, momentarily startled.

She stood there, face-to-face with Kale, neither one moving, neither one breathing. Dressed in a pair of jeans and a tight-fitting sweater, he looked as sexy as hell as he leaned against the doorjamb. He was so gorgeous, so hot she was sure he could liquefy metal. His bedroom blues dropped to examine her bare legs.

Her heart settled in her throat, and a prickle of awareness rushed through her as she in turn appraised him. He reached for her.

Without hesitation she accepted the offered hand and tangled her fingers though his, allowing him to pull her inside. He drew her close, close enough that she could smell the soapy clean scent of his skin as well as his spicy aftershave. The connection of body touching body was thrilling.

She immediately warmed as her breasts crushed against a wall of thick muscle. His midnight hair was slicked off his forehead and combed to the side, his face freshly shaven. He looked good enough to lick all over—like candy that had been coated with rich chocolate and dipped in spun sugar.

Warmth and familiarity rushed through her as she nestled against him. She didn't even try to curb the impulse to touch his smooth skin. With lust driving her actions, she ran her hand over his cheek, feathered her fingers over his jaw, and rested her head against his neck. She couldn't believe how much her body ached for him.

Thick muscles shifted as he pulled in a sharp breath. Her heart slammed against her chest as his gentle fingers moved to her cheeks. Boldly, she planted her pelvis against his and could feel his mounting desire.

He cupped her chin and lifted her eyes to his. His gaze was full of lust, but underneath that she detected tenderness and warmth. Some deeper emotion stirred inside her and tightened her chest. Feelings long ago restrained swam to the surface. She bit back the tug of emotions and pinched her eyes shut. It was disconcerting the way he engaged her emotionally.

She could understand the physical attraction between them, but it was the closeness she felt toward him that caused her great alarm.

God, what was she getting herself into? If she wasn't careful she could fall in love with him. Since he'd invited her over only for a night of wild, casual sex and nothing more, she had to get hold of her emotions. If she stuck around any longer, she'd surely lose her heart.

Kale took a small step back and eased open her coat. The smoldering look in his eyes as his gaze swept over her fiery red, body-molding dress excited her. Obviously, draining her checking account to purchase something so elaborate, something she'd likely never wear again, had been worth it.

"Hi." His voice was husky, throaty. "I've been waiting for you."

The eagerness in his tone excited her. He leaned in and planted a warm, gentle kiss on her cheek. His earthy, familiar male scent curled around her, making her feel so warm and comfortable.

He inched back and looked deep into her eyes as he brushed the pad of his thumb over her lips. "I'm so glad you came." The sincerity in his voice made her feel the way no other man had ever made her feel, cherished and important.

Something inside her shifted. She swallowed the lump clogging her throat. The tenderness in his voice sent a wave of possessiveness rushing through her. Emotions pulled her under like quicksand.

Oh boy!

She tamped down the tug of emotions, vowing to keep her feelings in check and this relationship impersonal.

"I came." Her voice sounded so breathless.

His grin turned wicked, his eyes full of teasing warmth. "Yes, you have. And you will again, and again."

Shivers of excitement raced through her as she caught the gist of his innuendo. As though leaving his mark on her, his hot thumb brushed roughly over her bottom lip. Her tongue followed behind his finger, tasting his warm, salty essence.

She opened her mouth to speak, but before she had a chance, he snaked his hands around her waist and anchored her to him once again.

His lips hovered inches from hers as he pushed her coat off her shoulders. His hungry gaze seemed to bore through her clothes and touch every inch of her naked body. As his glance moved over her, liquid heat poured through her body. A tingle skipped down her spine.

His eyes were full of emotion. "You look gorgeous." His voice was deep, intimate. He ran his finger over her cheek, her throat, and then lower to sculpt the pattern of her curves. His murmur of appreciation made her wet. Had she been wearing any panties, they'd have been soaked.

She drew a breath as she felt her resolve to keep this relationship impersonal weaken around the edges. She feared if she spent too much time in his arms, or his bed, she'd lose her heart to him forever. Then and there she knew it for certain, she'd never be able to be with him more than once.

"Kale, this can only be one night." Because heartbreak wasn't an option.

She heard a sound low in his throat. "Then you shouldn't have worn that dress." He guided her inside, shut the door, and draped her coat over the sofa.

"Then maybe I should take it off." She toyed with the thin spaghetti straps.

He gave a slow side-to-side shake of his head and removed her hands. "I don't think so." He brushed his thumb over her shoulders, using the same sensuous, stimulating circular strokes he'd used earlier on her clitoris.

She furrowed a brow as her body throbbed. "No?"

Holding her gaze, he slid his hand between her opened legs. "Uh-uh. I'll be doing that for you." When his fingers connected with her damp, silky curls, his eyes opened wide. His breath stalled. His nostrils flared. "Shit, Erin, you're not wearing any panties."

She shrugged innocently. "Laundry day, and I gave you my last clean pair." Liar. More like she wanted him to show her how he punished naughty girls. Of course, she wasn't about to admit that to him. At least not yet. Maybe later, though. She bit back a breathy moan as her body shook with anticipation.

The cords on his throat tightened as he swallowed. "How the fuck am I supposed to make it through dinner knowing you're naked under that dress?"

Her eyes opened wide, puzzled. "Dinner?"

He shifted his stance, obviously uncomfortable. He looked like he was in total agony. It really shouldn't have pleased her as much as it did. She just loved the way she affected him.

"Yeah, dinner. I cooked for you." His voice sounded strangled.

Her face softened. "You did?"

He drove his hands deep in his pockets. He looked so boyish, so adorable. An invisible band tightened around her heart.

"Yeah." His expression softened when his gaze fell over her.

She looked past him and noticed the dining room table. It was beautifully set for two. The sweet gesture tugged on her insides. Christmas candles burned in the center of the dinner table and perfumed the air. The flames flickered in the dimly lit room, casting mesmerizing, alluring shadows on the terra-cotta–colored walls.

"But I thought we were just going to have sex. Casual sex," she stressed, worry tugging at her insides.

Amusement pulled at the corners of his eyes. "Oh we are,

Erin," he assured her. "I just thought you might need fuel first. Now that I have you here, I don't plan on letting you go for a very long time." The deep timbre of his voice made her tremble. "I plan on beating that five-minute record of yours by at least two hours, maybe more."

"Oh," she said, her eyes opening wide.

He reached for her and guided her to the table. His large palm practically covered her entire hand. Keeping pace, she followed him into the dining room. She glanced around and couldn't believe that he'd gone to so much trouble to set the mood for seduction. Cloaked in semidarkness, the ambience was cozy, romantic, designed for lovers.

Lovers!

Her heart raced.

Suddenly that word made what they were about to do seem so personal, so intimate.

"Are you hungry?" He pulled her chair out and she graciously accepted.

She fought to recover her voice. "Yes." She neglected to tell him she'd grabbed a bite at the mall. He'd obviously gone to a lot of effort, and things were so perfect, she didn't want to spoil the moment.

The flames on the candles wavered as he took a seat beside her. His piercing blue eyes caught the light and shimmered. Everything about the room, about him, created an instant intimacy. The band around her heart tightened as she watched him settle next to her. She felt so warm, so close to him. She leaned into him and smiled. Something inside her compelled her to touch his hand. She *needed* the physical contact, as if her very next breath depended on it.

"Thank you for dinner. It smells delicious."

A wide grin split his face. His voice was low, mellow. "Do you like to cook, Erin?" He brushed his thumb over her skin with agonizing gentleness and gazed so deep into her eyes, she was sure he could touch her soul and read her every secret. Heat radiated from his hands and stirred her insides. It wasn't the way her body reacted to his touch that had her concerned, it was the way her heart reacted.

She pulled back, cursing herself for feeling so emotional. Taking a moment to regroup, she reminded herself this was just about casual sex. Nothing more. Nothing less.

"Not if I don't have to." It wasn't a complete lie. All-talk-and-no-action Erin Shay might be a closet domestic, but this new version of her, bad-girl Erin Shay, didn't enjoy making quiche, omelets, or even breakfast frittatas. The less personal things were between them, the easier it would be for her to walk away.

"Then I guess I'm in charge of breakfast too."

Comprehension and unease hit her at the same time. She realized what he meant. He wanted her to stay over.

Oh hell!

As Kale gazed at her from across the table, tightness settled in his chest. It was almost impossible to look away from her beauty. There was no denying that Erin stirred him both physically and emotionally, and was everything he'd been looking for. Everything he needed.

Sure he could have skipped the meal and jumped straight in the sack with her, but he wanted more. He wanted to talk with her, to get to know her on a deeper level, and to find out why she kept herself so guarded. He wanted to discover what horrible incident from her past had left her so jaded when it came to men and relationships.

"Everything looks beautiful, Kale." She glanced into the living room. "You even put up a tree. It's gorgeous."

Her voice pulled his mind from its wanderings. "Thank you." He glanced at her, his gaze moving over her features. The candlelight emphasized her sculpted cheekbones and bronzed skin. Her nutmeg hair was clipped at her nape. Dark hooded eyes brimmed with unleashed passion.

He could lose himself in those eyes. Come to think of it, he already had.

The love he felt for her suddenly blew over him like a gale force wind, leaving him feeling unstable and light-headed.

He drew a quick rejuvenating breath and poured her a glass of white wine. As he watched her take a small sip, it took all his restraint not to swipe his arm across the table, clear it of its contents, and make sweet love to her right there. All night long.

"Delicious," she said, licking the last drop from her plump lips. She looked past his shoulders into the kitchen. "What smells so good?"

He cleared his throat. "I thought we'd start with a shrimp appetizer."

She twirled her glass in her fingers. "What, no oysters?" she teased playfully.

He chuckled, loving her playful side. "I don't need them." He drained the wine from his glass and leaned into her. He glanced pointedly at her pert nipples. "Do you?"

"No," she admitted honestly.

"Good." Standing, he turned his back to her and disappeared into the kitchen.

"Do you need any help?" Erin called out.

"Nope. Stay put."

A moment later he came back carrying a shrimp platter and dipping sauce. He positioned them in the center of the table and reclaimed his chair.

"Looks great," Erin said.

After he seated himself, Erin reached for a shrimp but he quickly stopped her. He closed his hand over hers, the pad of his thumb rubbing her flesh. The sweet friction almost made him skip the meal and give in to his urges.

"Allow me," he said, trying to keep his voice level.

She tucked her hands into her lap as he dipped the shrimp into the seafood sauce and slowly carried it to her mouth. She parted her pretty cinnamon-painted lips, and he placed it on her tongue.

"Mmmm. Delicious." She nibbled and moaned a sweet, sexy bedroom moan that made his groin ache. It was the same noise she'd made when she orgasmed in the elevator and in the research room. Fuck. If she kept it up he'd never be able to think coherently or hold a civil conversation.

He lowered his voice and sidled closer. "What we did on the elevator today was really incredible, Erin."

Her eyes glistened. "Yeah, I know." Her voice was breathy, intimate.

"You were such a bad girl." He leaned in and whispered in her ear. "You were very wild. And hot."

Her eyes darkened with heat and passion. "You too."

She reached for the platter. "My turn." She dipped the shrimp into the sauce and seductively carried it to him. He leaned into her and drew it into his mouth. As he chewed, he watched her reach for another shrimp. She covered it in a generous amount of sauce and poised it near her sensuous lips.

Kale's gaze dropped to her cleavage. "You dripped sauce on yourself."

Her eyes glistened and caressed him with sultry heat. Her chin lifted a notch, challenging him. "Maybe I did it on purpose." She popped the shrimp into her mouth. Her pink tongue slid over her fleshy lips as she chewed.

He cocked his head, intrigued. "Yeah?" He watched her pulse beat at the creamy base of her neck. That's where he wanted his mouth.

She stared at him for an endless moment, then spread her legs in a silent message. "All that talk about licking today got me thinking."

Oh hell, forget the meal. He could no longer stave off the urgent demands of his body or fight the inevitable. They'd talk later, after he'd made love to her, when they were snuggled under the sheets.

Deciding to play along with her seductive game, he let his eyes leave her face and slowly track downward to settle on her distended nipples. Oh yeah, shrimp was the last thing he was interested in popping into his mouth.

"What are you thinking about?" He watched the seafood sauce trickle down her flesh as sparks shot through his body.

She looked at him with pure desire. "That maybe you could come over here and lick it off."

His heart almost failed as a jolt of desire fired through his blood. He could hardly believe how bold, how wild she really was.

She pushed the plate away and arched into him. One sexy brow rose. "I'm hungry, Kale. But not for shrimp." Her voice had taken on a raspy edge.

His body moistened. His cock throbbed. He was on his feet in less than a second. His chair went clattering to the floor. Damned if he didn't love a woman who knew what she wanted.

She drew her bottom lip between her teeth, dipped a hand under her dress, and stroked. "I believe you promised to make me scream."

Chapter 8

With predatory movements, Kale kicked his chair out of the way and came toward her. Erin's pulse leaped in her throat as he inched closer. She braced herself against her seat. God, he was so hot, so feral. His every movement was seductive, arousing, and heart-stopping.

He gripped her wooden seat, eased her chair away from the table, and sank to his knees until they were eye to eye. He urged her thighs farther apart and insinuated himself in between.

"Maybe we'd better get this dress off you before you spill sauce on it." Equal amounts of fear and excitement coiled through her when she heard the dark desire in his voice.

Without breaking eye contact, she reached up and touched her fingers to the thin spaghetti straps. The quick shake of his head stopped her.

"Don't," he commanded in a gentle voice. "Like I said earlier, I'll take care of that for you."

Kale twirled the straps in his fingers and slowly drew them down until he exposed the milky swell of her cleavage. She listened as his breathing hitched.

"I've lost sleep over your gorgeous breasts," he said. He tugged the dress until it fell to her waist. Sitting back on his heels, he took his sweet time to gaze at her dark, engorged nipples.

Erin cupped both her breasts, kneaded them gently, and ran her fingers over her hard, protruding nipples in an effort to ease the sexual ache.

A deep growl sounded low in his throat as he watched her pleasure herself. "You are so naughty, Erin." Grabbing both her hands, he held them hostage at her sides. A shudder rippled through her as he nuzzled his face close to her cleavage. She threw her head back and moaned. Her skin grew tight as she waited for him to close his mouth over her puckered mounds. The first touch of his velvety, talented tongue sent fire spiraling through her.

With excruciating gentleness he licked one plump nipple, tasting it, savoring it, teasing it until it tightened painfully in his mouth. He ran the puckered bud across his teeth, nipping until she gasped in pleasure and pain. She squirmed, wanting more, wanting him to answer all the urgent demands in her quaking body.

The ache between her legs grew until the sensations overtook her. She pulled her hands free from his and tore at his sweater. Kale lifted his arms, allowing her to pull it off. His chest was magnificent, just as she knew it would be. She stroked and massaged his hard pectorals. Edging closer, she flicked her tongue out and circled his tightening nipple. His muscles convulsed and bunched under her tongue. She could feel his heart pound against his chest. The fast, erratic rhythm matched her own.

She'd never been so hot, so turned on, in her entire life. She put her lips over his and whispered, "Take me to your bedroom. I want to have sex with you on the bed you've been sleeping in."

"Follow me." He grabbed her hands and pulled her to her feet. It took a moment for her to figure out how to walk again. Kale hustled her down the hallway, pushed open his bedroom door, and pulled her inside. The light from the hallway spilled in, bathing the bed in warm, sensual hues. The scent of his aftershave hung in the air. As she stepped over the threshold, her gaze was drawn to the unmade bed. Visions of herself writhing for him, the way he liked, on those unkempt sheets made her ache deep between her legs.

He circled his arms around her waist and pushed his erection against her. "Do you know how much I want you?" His voice was tangled with emotion.

"Yes." She reached out and placed her hand over his impressive bulge and massaged. "I'd say about as much as I want you." She positioned her pelvis against his, right where it counted.

He groaned and gyrated against her. "You are so fucking wild."

"You make me this way." She'd never before been so bold or aggressive. She liked this side of herself. She liked the confidence he brought out in her.

Kale gripped the sides of her dress and dropped to his knees. He tugged, pulling the dress to her ankles. His face was only inches from the seat of her desire.

He trailed his fingers over her calves. "Lift your legs for me, babe."

She stepped out of the dress, and Kale tossed it aside.

His gaze locked with hers as his large hands touched her inner thigh. His blue eyes were so very dark, so richly seductive. She instinctively widened her stance.

"I've been dying to taste you. It's all I could think about since the minute we met." His warm breath caressed her swollen folds. He buried his face between her legs and licked all the way from the back to the front, lapping at her syrupy arousal. She moaned and quaked as his thumb climbed higher and higher until he stroked her swollen clitoris.

He eased back, licked his lips, and groaned appreciatively. "You taste better than candy."

Her heart beat in a mad rush as her whole body turned to liquid. She raked her fingers though his hair. "My legs. I can't stand anymore."

Kale stood and gathered her into his embrace. She wound her arms around his neck as he carried her to the bed. With smooth efficiency he laid her across his tousled cotton bedding. His masculine scent permeated the rumpled sheets. She inhaled deeply, basking in the arousing aroma as it filled her with anticipation.

He stood beside the bed and went to work on his jeans. After he removed them he tore off his shorts and kicked them aside. His huge cock sprang free, clamoring for attention. Her gaze moved over his awe-inspiring body. He was so beautiful. An equal measure of excitement and nervousness rushed through her as she watched his magnificent arousal throb and thicken. Her mouth salivated. She swallowed. Hard.

"Come to me." She reached for him, urging him to join her on the bed.

Balancing his arm beside her head, he pushed his erection against her hip and sank into her mouth. She drew his tongue in to mate with hers. His hot velvet tongue moved inside her mouth, hungry, restless. She could taste her creamy essence on his lips.

She wrapped her legs around his thighs and rubbed her damp sex against him. Reaching down, she sheathed his cock in her hand. He moaned when she slid her hand up and down the length of his shaft. He pulsed in her palm, his veins becoming engorged with blood.

He sucked in a breath and flinched. "Don't."

"Why?" she asked, feigning innocence even though she already knew the answer to that question.

"I'll lose it, and I'm not ready to. I haven't finished with you yet," he rasped.

Kale rolled onto his back and pulled her on top of him. The floor-length mirror seemed to catch his eyes. His grin turned wicked. She shivered with excitement, wondering what other fantasy he had in mind.

"I want you on your knees with your legs spread for me," he whispered into Erin's ear.

That excited her. "Is this another one of your fantasies?" she asked.

He nodded and smiled that bad-boy smile of his that made her insides melt and her heart turn over.

After he helped her to her knees, Kale straddled her from behind. "You were very naughty for not wearing underwear tonight," he said, cupping her chin and turning it toward the mirror. "And I told you how I punish naughty girls." He whacked her ass.

"Oh my," Erin whispered breathlessly. The slap stung, but she liked it. A lot.

He pitched his voice low and put his mouth near her ear. "You understand I need to punish you, Erin."

"Oh yes, I understand," she said eagerly, wiggling in anticipation.

He slapped her with an open palm. Harder this time, leaving her backside warm and wanting. Her knees quivered and buckled beneath her. Had it not been for Kale's chest pressed against her back, she would have collapsed in a quivering heap.

After another slap, her legs wobbled. Not wanting to break the erotic moment, she fought to remain upright. When his hand connected again, waves of hot desire rushed through her, turning her limbs to pudding.

"I don't know if I can stay like this," she murmured, not wanting him to stop but needing him to hold her tightly, to prevent her from toppling over.

He anchored her to him, supporting her. "I've got you," he whispered gently.

God, he was so in tune with her emotions, her needs. Her insides turned to putty. She was amazed at the intensity of feelings he brought out in her. For a brief moment she wondered what it would be like if he weren't leaving in a month. Wondered what it'd be like if this relationship wasn't about casual sex. Lord, what was it about him that made her begin to reevaluate dating and relationships?

He tightened his grip on her waist and held her against him while he ran his other hand down her neck and over her breast. He plucked at her swollen nipples. Erin began to pant as his fingers inched lower. Staring at each other in the mirror, their eyes met and locked.

"Spread farther for me."

Erin opened her legs as wide as they would go and arched into him.

"I can smell your arousal, Erin."

Eyes fluttering shut, she moaned and wiggled her backside against him. He growled and pressed his cock between her ass cheeks.

His fingers brushed her damp, curly locks before parting her dewy folds. As he exposed her pink, swollen pebble in the mirror, her eyes darkened with heat. He flicked her delicate nub and pinched it between his thumb and fore-finger.

"Oh God, Kale, that feels so good." She reached behind her in search of his erection.

He inched away. "Oh no, you don't. You must watch." He tilted her head forward again. "This is also part of your pun-ishment. You only get to watch. There will be no touching or tasting for you. Only for me."

"That's not fair," she whimpered her protests, meeting his gaze in the mirror.

"I don't play fair. I thought you would have figured that out by now." He stroked her with the lightest caress and she nearly exploded into a million pieces. "Tell me what you want," he whispered, his warm breath caressing her neck, making her wild with need.

She began panting. "I want you to make me scream, like you promised."

He chuckled, his warm breath stimulating her flesh. "Are you hot and wet for me?"

She nodded eagerly.

"You'd better be. If I lower my finger and dip into you only to find out that you're not dripping wet, you'll be pun-ished even more." His eyes flashed with dark, hot passion. God, he looked so wild, so out of control.

"I am wet, see for yourself." She whimpered and wiggled her backside over his groin, hoping to make him as wild as he was making her. He groaned.

Pleasure Prolonged

Deliberately slow, he toyed with her, dragging his finger lower, but never touching where she needed it the most.

Her eyes pleading, she met his glance in the mirror. He was killing her with his slow seduction. "Please, Kale. Touch me. I ache so much, I *need* you to touch me before I go up in flames," she begged, feeling insanely open and honest with him. She'd never been comfortable enough with anyone to voice her body's needs, her heart's desires.

Kale growled and honored her request as he dipped two fingers in her.

She felt her pussy clamp over his fingers as he pushed deep inside her. She closed her eyes and drew in a ragged breath, savoring the exquisite feel of him moving in and out, slowly, steadily.

In no time at all, she could feel her orgasm pulling at her as he kept up the gentle assault. He was raising her passion to new heights just as she'd known he would. Taking matters into his own hands, giving her what she needed instead of worrying only about his own pleasure.

Her head lolled to the side. "You always know how to touch me just right." She bucked against his hand and felt the wet tip of his arousal against her flesh. "When do I get to touch you?" she asked, breathless.

"Soon, Erin, but right now this is about you."

He worked his fingers in her as his lips scorched her skin with heated kisses. Her muscles began to clench and undulate. She was on the edge, ready to fall over. Erin cupped her breasts and squeezed, knowing ecstasy was merely a stroke or two away. Moments before she felt herself tumble into euphoria, he removed his fingers.

"No . . ." she protested. "Don't stop."

"I don't plan on it," he murmured.

He shimmied between her legs until she was straddling his mouth. He gripped her hips and eased her onto his face where he replaced his fingers with his tongue. His thumb circled higher until he touched her fleshy clitoris. Using small circles, he toyed with her hard nub until she lost her grip on sanity. He pushed his hot tongue deep inside her, stroking her inner fire until that first sweet clench of fulfillment took hold.

Erin cried out as a powerful orgasm rolled over her. She writhed over his mouth and ran her fingers through his hair. "That's *so* good."

He continued to work his tongue over her sex as she rode out her orgasm. "I want to feel you inside me," she cried, bucking against him. He cupped her bottom in his hands and held her in place. "Please, Kale, let me slide down and put your cock inside me."

"Soon," Kale assured her. "I just need to finish tasting your sweetness first." He feathered his tongue over her pussy with long, luxurious strokes. His tongue felt rough against her overly sensitive clitoris. Once again her muscles began to tighten and swell in bliss.

She palmed her breasts. "Oh God, Kale. I'm going to come again."

"That's the plan." He pushed two fingers deep inside her

and applied just the right amount of pressure to her clitoris as she tumbled into her second orgasm of the night.

After Kale had his fill of her sweetness, he rolled her onto the bed beside him. Warmth flooded her as she touched his cheek. He twisted his head and brushed his lips over her palm.

When their eyes met, something intimate seeped under her skin and curled around her heart. Erin blew out a shaky breath and swallowed.

"Kale," she whispered breathlessly, rubbing her palm over his face. Her voice lodged somewhere deep in her throat.

"Erin ..." The way he said her name instantly brought them to a deeper level of intimacy. He leaned into her hand. "I love the way you touch me," he said. The soft timbre of his voice filled her with solace. When he smiled at her, her heart turned over in her chest.

A cocoon of warmth encompassed her. "And I love the way you touch me," she returned, acknowledging the rush of emotions turning her insides to jelly.

"That's good, because I'm far from done." He smoothed her hair back and looked deep into her eyes. He pitched his voice low. "Let me grab a condom."

She nodded in agreement. "Hurry, Kale. I don't want to wait another second for you to make love to me." Her voice was husky with emotion.

Make love.

Oh God!

This wasn't sex. This was lovemaking. She wasn't naïve enough to believe otherwise.

Nervousness stole over her. Common sense would have dictated she get dressed and run away from him, but since common sense wasn't ruling her actions, she remained sprawled across his bed. Wide open and vulnerable.

Kale turned sideways and grabbed a condom from his nightstand. She glided her fingers over his back as he ripped the foil package open. With skilled efficiency, he rolled it down the length of his erection.

He turned back to face her. When his gaze locked with hers, she felt so close to him. She wanted to crawl inside him and stay there forever. She swallowed past the lump in her throat.

"Did you want to be on top, babe?"

She felt tightness in her chest, a little to the left. "It doesn't matter, Kale. I just want to feel you inside me."

He rolled on top of her and situated himself between her legs. Blood pounded through her veins as his erection probed her slick opening. She thrust her hips forward, forcing his cock to press against her passion-drenched cleft.

He growled, his breath fanning her face. He looked at her with pure desire. "Next time, you can be on top. I want to take you like this for now so I can hold you close and kiss you."

Next time.

There wasn't supposed to be a next time.

She made a sexy noise and shifted, bending her legs at the knees, welcoming him into her body. His mouth closed over hers for a soul-stirring kiss as he buried himself in her. The tantalizing sweep of his velvety rough tongue inside her mouth made her shudder.

Pleasure Prolonged

Heat coursed through her as she wound her hands around his neck and held him close. His thickness pushed open the tight walls of her throbbing pussy. She felt so deliciously full.

He lifted his lips a fraction of an inch from hers and growled into her mouth. "Ahhh, you feel so incredible." His breathing was labored as he began thrusting. At first his movements were slow and gentle, but when she lifted her hips off the bed to meet his every push, he began pumping harder and faster.

She could feel her orgasm building as his cock caressed her oversensitized hot spot. Her head fell to the side as the pressure grew. She began panting, gasping for her next breath.

Kale buried his mouth in the crook of her neck. A strangled cry sounded deep in his throat as he kissed, licked, and nibbled on her flesh.

Slick moisture pooled on their naked flesh as need consumed them both. She pushed Kale's damp hair from his forehead and writhed beneath him. His cock pulsed and throbbed inside her, and she knew he was only a heartbeat away from finding his own release.

"Kale, I'm …"

"I know, babe, me too."

Her senses exploded with the sudden onslaught of pleasure as her orgasm took hold. She dug her fingers into Kale's back and arched off the bed.

His breath came in a ragged burst as he exploded inside her. She tightened her sex muscles around his cock, milking every last drop from him. They held each other for a long, quiet moment, both needing time to recoup and recover from their mind-blowing sex.

He inched back and gazed deep into her eyes. "You're so beautiful," he whispered, breaking the comfortable silence encompassing them.

She cupped his cheeks and brought his mouth close to hers. She drew a shaky breath and moistened her lips. "God, Kale, that was so . . . so incredible. "I've never—"

He cut her off. "Gone past five minutes?"

She chuckled. "Yeah, that too. But I've never had so many orgasms in one day before."

He brushed her hair from her face and planted a soft kiss onto her forehead. A kiss so full of emotion and tenderness, she wanted to weep.

His mouth twisted and he gave a soft chuckle. His laugh wrapped around her like her favorite cotton robe. She felt so safe, so cherished. So complete. She wanted to stay in the circle of his arms forever.

"Hold that thought, babe. I'm not done with you yet," he murmured.

She raised her gaze to his. When she looked deep into his smoldering blue eyes, she felt a possessive tug on her heart. God, she could drown in those eyes. She swallowed hard and pushed down the wave of emotions. "I'm not done with you either. Come with me."

"Where?"

She grinned. "You're not the only one with fantasies."

Chapter 9

Sweat beaded on his forehead as life surged into his cock. What was the little vixen up to?

"I'll be right back." He made a quick trip to the bathroom to dispense with the condom. After cleaning himself up, he came back with a warm cloth for her. Erin sat on the edge of the bed, waiting for him.

"I thought you might want this." He dropped to his knees, urged her thighs apart, and caressed her swollen sex with the cloth.

"Oh my," she moaned. As she blew out a breath, her silken curls shuddered. "Is that supposed to be turning me on?"

Kale grinned. "You really are a bad girl, aren't you, Erin?"

She returned his grin. "You ain't seen nothin' yet." She reached for his hand. "Come with me."

Kale stood. "I'll *come* with you anytime, anywhere," he whispered, a faint tinge of humor in his voice.

She made a quick trip to the bathroom and grabbed a couple of oversized towels, then guided him to the patio doors off the dining room.

She tossed him a towel. "Wrap yourself. It's cold out there."

Erin pulled her thick terry towel over her bare shoulders.

He cocked a brow. "We're going out there? Naked?"

She nodded.

"Is your fantasy to freeze me to death?"

Standing on her tiptoes, she leaned into him and pressed her lips over his. Her breasts grazed his chest. He loved how free and uninhibited she was with him.

"Hot tub," she murmured into his mouth.

Understanding finally dawned on him. How in the hell had he forgotten about the hot tub?

Erin inched open the door. Before she could make a run for it the doorbell sounded, stopping them both in their tracks.

Kale glanced at the clock and noted it was nearing eight. He wasn't expecting anyone. He furrowed his brow. "Who could that be?"

Erin shrugged. "I don't know."

"Should we ignore it?"

Erin hugged her towel tighter. "I think we should answer. It could be something important for Jay or Laura."

Kale nodded in agreement. "You're probably right. Let's grab a robe." He turned to face the door. "I'll be right there," he called out. He grabbed Erin's hands in his and put his mouth close to hers. His eyes darkened as he whispered, "Then we'll finish what we started."

After they each pulled on a thick terry robe, Erin went and sat on the sofa in front of the Christmas tree while Kale made his way to the front door. He pulled it open and came face-to-face with a UPS courier. In one hand he held a padded manila envelope, in the other an electronic signature device.

"Are you Kale Alexander?" the man asked.

"Yes," Kale answered, confused. Who would be sending him a package here, tonight?

"Sign here, please."

Kale signed and accepted the padded envelope. As he made his way to the sofa, he turned the package over in his hand and looked for some indication of its origin but found no return address. "This is strange."

Erin twisted around to face him. "What is it?"

Kale tore into the package and produced a computer disk. He ripped off the sticky note attached to it. "It comes with instructions to view right away."

"Who sent it?" Erin asked.

Kale shrugged. "I have no idea. Come on, Jay's computer is in his office. Let's go check it out."

Erin grabbed the envelope and examined the package and the metered postage. "This looks like it's from the lab."

Seating himself, Kale inserted the disk while Erin stood behind him, watching over his shoulder.

A few key strokes later a blurred video image appeared

on the screen. Brow furrowed, Kale angled his head and squinted. "What the hell am I watching?" As the image focused, understanding dawned. "Holy fuck," he bit out and nearly fell off his chair.

Erin gasped. "Ohmigod."

He twisted around to see her. Her face paled, her hands flew to her mouth. "Ohmigod," she repeated.

Kale jumped from the chair. Shock segued to rage as he watched a digital slide show of Erin writhing beneath him in the research room while he brought her to orgasm. "Who the hell . . ." His gut clenched, along with his fists.

He jabbed the eject button and tore the disk from the computer. He spun back around to face Erin. Eyes open wide, she stood there, slack jawed, staring at the blank screen.

"Erin, what the hell is going on?"

She reached for the envelope and fished around inside until she produced a note. As she scanned the words, her face paled even more.

"Ohmigod," she repeated, and held the paper out for him. "Lab . . . recorder . . . still running . . . director . . . distracted . . . forgot to turn off . . . Hooker Barbie . . . watching me . . . pink camper . . . run her over." Her words were fractured and she wasn't making sense. He was definitely missing something.

Kale dropped the disk onto the desk and grabbed the paper from her hand. He read it once, and then a second time. "Jesus H. Christ."

"Shit. Shit. Shit," Erin blurted out, pressing the butts of her palms to her eyes. "Stupid. Stupid. Stupid." She turned her back to him and paced toward the door. "My list of people to kill just grew by one."

"Where are you going?" He closed the small distance between them, grabbed her by the waist, and turned her back around.

"You read the note. If I don't step down, Hooker Barbie is going to send a copy of this to the director." She rubbed her temple and mumbled another round of curses. "Playing sex games in the research room during work hours isn't going to get me that promotion, Kale. It's going to get me fired."

"Who the hell is Hooker Barbie?"

"Deanne Sinclair. She wants my job. Obviously." This was turning out to be some pissing contest.

He scoffed and shook his head. "I had my own run-in with her. And it wasn't my *job* she was after." The details of the encounter weren't worth mentioning.

She closed her eyes in distress and then nodded toward the paper. "What does she mean, you're on probationary status?"

Kale let out a long sigh. "A few months back I fucked up at Castech, and if I fuck up again, I'm out of a job." He scrubbed his hand over his jaw. "Apparently Deanne's been busy, doing a little research of her own. She's been digging into my confidential records."

"Like Deanne said, if I don't step down, I'll be dragging you with me. And I'm not about to do that." She got quiet for a moment and then added, "Talk about one hell of a bump in the road, Kale. I guess this is your exit."

The significance of her actions didn't elude him. Erin was willing to give up her career, the one thing that meant the world to her, to save his. A sudden rush of warmth enveloped him as his heart tightened in his chest. No woman had ever done anything so meaningful, so touching for him before. His chest swelled as the love he felt for her grew to insurmountable proportions.

"What are you talking about, Erin? I'm not going to let you step down."

Her tongue darted over her lips, moistening them. Her eyes opened wide as surprise registered on her face. "You will if you want to save your own ass."

"Fuck my ass. Wait." He shook his head, flustered. "That came out all wrong."

Perplexed, she looked at him. "This is your out, Kale. Why would you go down with me when you don't have to?"

He hauled her into the circle of his arms. "Unless it's in the bedroom, sweetheart, neither one of us is going down. Besides, I take full responsibility for what happened this afternoon."

Dark eyes flashed with tumultuous emotions. Her chin came up a notch, astonished. Her voice was low. "A man who takes responsibility. That's so refreshing." She conjured a smile. "But you weren't the only one in that room, Kale."

Eyes riveted on hers, he dragged a finger over her chin, her cheek, and brushed her hair from her shoulders. "It doesn't matter. I'm the one who seduced you."

Erin arched a brow. "And here I thought it was the other way around."

He snaked his arms around her waist and held her tighter. "You worked your tail off for this position, and Hooker Bambi is not going to take it from you."

"Hooker Barbie," she corrected.

Hooker Bambi, Hooker Barbie, the name didn't matter. He knew her type all too well, had dealt with conniving women like her many times. He shook his head as he considered the situation a moment longer.

"I don't believe Deanne has any plans to take this to the director. The information stored on the digital video recorder is highly confidential. If she's tampered with it, or made copies"—he reached behind him, scooped up the copy she'd sent them, and held it up—"she'll be implicating herself."

"She could send it to him anonymously."

"I don't know how anonymous she thinks she can be. It is her job to record and log the responses from the digital data, isn't it?"

"Regardless, even if she's not bright enough to figure out she'll go down with me, I don't want a copy of this landing in the director's hands. Or on the Internet."

"I really don't think that's going to happen, Erin. Even on the net, it could be traced back to her. Trust me, I have dealt with her type many times. She's bluffing. I'd bet my last dollar on it. But if it will help ease your concern, I'll go to the lab and erase it from the hard drive."

Incredulous, Erin lifted her eyes to his. She swallowed. "Really? You'd do that?" Her voice wavered when she added, "For me?"

Everything in him reached out to her as her expressive gaze told him how much that offer surprised her, meant to her. He touched her cheek. "Of course."

She got quiet for a moment, and Kale wondered what she was thinking. Was she beginning to see them as more than casual? Was she beginning to trust him, to finally acknowledge there was more driving their relationship than just physical desire?

"And if she did make a copy?" Erin asked.

"If she did make a copy I'll get that too."

"How?" she asked, her expression wary.

His mind raced a mile a minute as he considered things a moment longer. "She mailed this from the lab, right?"

Erin nodded.

"Probably because she didn't want to get caught leaving with confidential office documentation." Kale tapped the disk. "I'm also willing to bet if she did make another copy, it's stored in her locker. She wouldn't want to have it in her possession outside the center."

"So how do we get into her locker?"

"I break in."

When her head came up with a start, he presented her with a cocky grin and said, "Misguided youth."

Erin scoffed. "You're charming, Kale. Charming enough to talk your way out the eye of a hurricane, but I don't think that charm will work on the nighttime security if you get caught in Deanne's locker. You're not Gerard's type."

"That's where you come in."

Her eyes opened wide, questioning him. "Go on," she said.

He wrapped his arms around her and pulled her close, until every inch of her body was pressed up against him. When her sensuous body melded with his, he trembled. "We'll have to rely on one another if we want to pull this off."

She looked at him, her eyes wide, questioning. "Enlighten me."

He brushed her cheek with the pad of his thumb. He felt her shiver in response. Obviously their proximity was affecting her as much as him.

"Are you able to have faith in me, Erin?" His stomach clenched as he waited for her response.

He sensed her hesitation. "Yes."

Kale's stomach relaxed. "Good. Now go put on that sexy dress of yours. You have some distracting to do."

Erin's heart raced like she'd been given a shot of adrenaline as Kale escorted her into the front lobby. Maneuvering across the wide expanse of floor, he pressed his hand against the small of her back as they moved toward the security counter. God, she loved the way he touched her in such an intimate way.

Nervousness began stealing over her as they approached Gerard. Although he was used to seeing her coming and going at odd hours, and her presence tonight wouldn't raise his suspicions, she still felt jittery.

She strove for normalcy as she greeted him. "Good evening, Gerard." She glanced at the security screen behind him and watched it flash in an indistinguishable pattern as it displayed secure areas of the lab.

His nod was tight and very professional. "Good evening, Erin, Kale."

Erin cringed inwardly. If only Mikey were working the night shift. Gerard wasn't the flirty type. Mikey would have been much easier to distract while Kale broke into Barbie's locker.

"We have to grab a file. We're working late," Erin explained as she unbuttoned her coat and eased it open, exposing her sexy dress.

When Gerard caught sight of her barely there, hot red slip of a dress, his forehead creased. He shot her a suspicious look and raised a brow as if to say, *You're going to work late in that?* Damn, that wasn't the reaction she'd been going for.

When she met his steely gaze, her stomach plummeted. She didn't like this. God, she really didn't. Not one tiny bit.

Erin smiled and pushed back her panic. "First we have a quick Christmas gathering to attend, then we have to go over some paperwork before tomorrow morning's experiment."

Satisfied with her answer, Gerard relaxed his forehead.

Trying for slutty, Erin leaned against the counter while Kale signed himself in. "I'll just be a second," he said. "Erin, you might as well just wait here."

Despite all her best efforts to distract him, Gerard turned his attention back to the monitors as Kale made his way to the elevator.

Pleasure Prolonged

Shit!

She glanced around the lobby, looking for something, anything to talk about. If a man wasn't interested in a woman in a hot red dress, then what the hell was he interested in?

A man in a hot red dress? Cripes! Maybe she and Kale should have switched places.

Then it hit her. Sports. All men liked sports, right? Her father and two brothers-in-law spent their weekends glued to the television watching football. She'd caught a few games with Sam as well. Although she had to admit, she knew nothing about football and had watched only so she could admire all those hunks in their tight uniforms.

"So did you catch the game last night?"

His head went up with a start as he twisted around to face her. A wide smile softened his features. She watched, transfixed at how quickly his demeanor changed. Who knew football was so powerful?

"You watch football?" he asked. His eyes opened wide with a mixture of surprise and admiration.

Erin linked her fingers and pretended to crack them. "Sure do. So what did you think of the game?"

Face animated, he started into a long, boring spiel about the Packers' kick-ass game last night. Erin plastered on her most expressive, enthusiastic face. It wasn't easy to feign interest, especially when he broke down the plays in detail and began laughing about the antics of some Cheeseheads.

Apparently, from his long-winded explanation, she surmised

the fans were called Cheeseheads. And men thought women's things were stupid. She resisted the urge to roll her eyes.

Ten minutes later she almost wished she hadn't brought up football. Hands waving wildly, he gave a detailed description about some quarterback named Favre and the amazing touchdown pass he made. Gerard was practically salivating. Lord, the man looked like he was in love.

Now if only he'd salivated over her dress like that, she wouldn't have to stand there all doe-eyed, faking interest. Eventually Gerard was going to get a clue and figure out she knew nothing about the game.

As he droned on, Erin inconspicuously stole a few glances at the monitor behind him.

So far so good.

She really should make an effort to add to the conversation, but what was she supposed to talk about, all those beefy guys and their tight little buns? She doubted he'd find the humor in it.

Restless, Erin shifted her stance. Gerard noticed the edgy movement. The way he quickly switched back to his professional mode and shot a glance at the monitors threw her off guard.

He arched a brow. "Kale seems to be taking an awfully long time."

Erin straightened. "Speak of the devil," she said, gesturing with her head. She turned her attention back to Gerard. "Nice talking with you." She raised her fists like pom-poms and yelled. "Go Packers, go!"

As Kale moved into the lobby, she pushed away from the counter and started toward him. Kale turned to her, a crooked smile on his handsome face. "What the hell was that?" he asked as they made their way to the doors.

She lowered her voice. "Don't ask." As soon as they exited the building, Erin turned to him. "Did you delete it from the hard drive? Did you get into her locker? Were there any copies?" she rushed out.

"Yes, yes, and one. And it's been taken care of." Kale circled the truck and opened the passenger side door for her. "We don't have anything to worry about, Erin. If she threatens you again, we've got the disk at my place to prove she's tampered with highly confidential material and removed it from the lab."

Elated that her job was no longer in jeopardy, Erin wrapped her arms around his neck and hugged him tight. She became acutely aware of the way her breasts crushed into a wall of tight muscle. "Thank you, Kale."

Chuckling, he hugged her back and lifted her feet off the ground. After he set her back down, he pulled back an inch but didn't let her go. He brought his mouth close to hers. "You're welcome," he whispered.

As she stood there, mouth poised open, body enclosed in the circle of his arms, waiting for him to kiss her, a bevy of emotions rushed through her. What he'd done for her tonight, the way he had supported her, even risked his own career to do it, touched her so deeply it rattled her right down to her toes. Instead of taking the next exit when they'd encountered a bump in the road, he'd stood by her and supported her. He had no idea how much that mattered to her.

There was so much more to this man than she had expected. When she decided to indulge in a casual affair with playboy Kale Alexander, she hadn't anticipated that she'd fall so hard for him. She swallowed the lump clogging her throat and cursed herself for feeling so emotional.

She put her palm flat against his face and spent an extra moment just looking at him. Her breath hitched. Cripes, what in the hell had she been thinking? Kale wasn't the kind of guy she could have a casual affair with, and she wasn't the kind of girl who could love casually. She ached for something far more intimate from him.

As his lips closed over hers, she knew it better than she knew her own name. Her simple plan to have a frivolous affair had backfired.

She was in way over her head.

Chapter *10*

Silence fell over them as Kale negotiated his truck into traffic. He stole a sideways glace at Erin. Fingers linked together, she rotated her thumbs in a tight circle and stared at the dark road ahead.

"Everything okay?" he asked.

Without looking his way, she nodded.

He closed his hand over hers and squeezed. "What are you thinking about?" he prodded.

She turned to face him. A flurry of emotions passed through her eyes. "Nothing." Her voice was low and a little edgy.

"Really? You weren't thinking about coming back to my place to tell me about this hot tub fantasy of yours?" he teased, hoping to lighten her mood.

She grinned. "That might have passed through my mind a time or two. Or a million," she said playfully.

Kale chuckled and squeezed her hand more tightly.

As they drove toward Kale's place, Erin got quiet again. She pointed to a side street and sighed. "I'm supposed to be there tonight."

"Your mother's? I didn't realize she lived so close to Jay and Laura."

She nodded and let out a slow breath. "It's a great place to raise kids. Laura had that in mind when she chose this location." She angled her chin. "Look at how well I turned out growing up in the burbs."

He furrowed his brow as his gaze panned her body. "Hmmm . . . Perhaps I'll have to have a chat with Jay before he decides to have children."

Erin whacked him and laughed. "Hey," she said. "You take that back."

Kale tapped the brakes and turned the truck around. He pulled down the side street that Erin had pointed to.

"What are you doing?" she asked, her voice rising an octave.

The parked cars on the curb gave away the location of her parents' house. He flicked a glance past Erin's shoulder and registered every detail of the impressive two-story home.

The truth was, Kale was anxious to meet Erin's family, to step into her private world. He wanted to glimpse this intimate side of her and take this relationship to the next level, where things were far more personal.

He pulled up behind one of the vehicles, shifted into park, and removed the keys. Distracting her, he sidled closer and put his mouth close to hers. A rush of sexual energy hit him as his lips touched her skin. "I'll take it back on one condition," he whispered. He inched back, his gaze shifting to her mouth.

Her heavy lids fluttered. "What's that?"

"You kiss me." His voice was husky with desire.

She wet her bottom lip. "I think that can be arranged."

A muscle in his jaw flexed. "Did I say one condition?" His lips touched hers ever so lightly. She moaned and leaned into him.

"Yes," she murmured into his mouth.

As he smoothed her hair from her face, sexual sparks leaped between them. He crowded her, sandwiching her between him and the door. Her body trembled beneath his.

"I meant two." His tongue traced the pattern of her sensuous mouth.

"Now you're pushing it." He heard the raw ache of lust in her voice.

He parted her lips with his tongue and dipped inside. "First you kiss me, then we'll go make a quick appearance at your parents' house, and after that we'll head back to my place so you can have your wicked way with me."

"Kale, I believe that was three conditions."

Hunger consumed him. "I don't think so, Erin. I just think you need to work on your math skills. I counted two."

"I don't think . . ." His head descended in time to smother her protest with a kiss.

He kissed her with all the passion inside him, until they were both forced to inch back to recapture their breath. Her cheeks were flushed, her eyes glossy and richly seductive.

He ran the pad of his thumb over her kiss-swollen lips. "So

what do you say, sweetheart. Want to go in?" He squeezed her hand, a silent message of support.

Breathless, she tripped over her words. "I'm not sure."

"We'll just make a quick appearance. I'll dazzle them with my charm, and then I'll take you back to my place and we'll discuss these fantasies of yours." He neglected to enlighten her as to his ulterior motives.

She starched her spine and mulled over the idea.

"Come on, Erin. Let's go get your mother off your back before she tries to marry you off to Donkey Kong boy."

He watched her resolve melt as she warmed to the idea. She crinkled her cute little nose. "Are you sure you really want to do this?"

"Yes."

She gave a resigned shake of her head. "You're very persuasive, Kale. Do you always get your own way?"

He cocked his head. "Always."

"I somehow suspected that."

"Come on, let's go." Kale climbed from the truck and circled around to meet her. He captured her hand in his as they made their way to the front door.

Erin sucked in air as she twisted the knob and stepped into the front entrance. Music and voices drifted out to them from the other room.

"In there," Erin said, her voice strangled.

They moved down the hall and turned the corner to the living room where guests stood around conversing, sipping champagne, and nibbling on hors d'oeuvres.

Her mother rushed forward when she caught sight of Erin. "You're late ..." Her voice fell off and she stopped dead in her tracks as her gaze went from Erin, to Kale, back to Erin again.

"Oh, I didn't realize you were bringing a ..." She paused as though carefully choosing her next word. She raised an inquisitive brow and finished the sentence. "Date?"

Erin squeezed his hand. Kale could feel her frustration. He squeezed her back, reassuring her, offering his comfort and support.

"Kale, this is my mom, Anna. Mom, this is Kale. He's my—"

Kale thrust his hand out and cut her off. His lips twitched. "I'm her boyfriend."

Taken aback, her mother shot Erin a glance as her elegantly manicured hand slipped inside Kale's. "Well, well, isn't this a surprise." A wide smile split her lips as she appraised Kale. "Where on earth did you find such a handsome man?"

Kale angled his head to face Erin. As they exchanged a look, something potent passed between them. "She didn't find me, I found her. And I consider myself damn lucky."

Anna turned her attention to Erin. "And when were you going to share this lovely man with the family?"

Share?

Erin's stomach churned. Didn't her mother know she wasn't into sharing? She wanted Kale. All to herself.

Oh boy!

Erin stood there, dazed, watching Kale turn on his play-boy charm and dazzle her mother with his quick wit, intoxi-cating good looks, and signature smile.

When he wrapped his arm around her, anchoring her to his side, her body began tingling in heated anticipation. She suddenly had a monumental craving for a hot fudge sundae.

As she watched him, her insides twisted. The word *boy-friend* rang in her ears. Of course, it was all part of the facade. Kale wasn't looking for anything long-term. He was into casual sex. He'd told her so himself. Which was the exact reason why she had decided to have an affair with him in the first place. He didn't want anything more from her. And now, by God, damned if she didn't want more from him.

Cripes, how was that for irony!

She closed her eyes against the flood of emotions. So much for "a hump and a bump, thank you chump." Now it was more like "a hump and a bump, I want it all chump!" A hus-band, children, and a quaint little house in suburbia.

As her mother engaged Kale in conversation, Erin took that opportunity to pull herself together. She caught sight of her father. He gave her a knowing, apologetic look. She smiled back, smoothed her bangs off her forehead, and tried to quiet her heartbeat. Striving for some semblance of con-trol, she glanced around the room, taking stock. Apparently Donkey Kong boy had chickened out. He was nowhere to be found. She gave a silent prayer of thanks.

Her mother took Kale's arm in hers. "Come on, Kale. Let

me introduce you to the guests." She turned back to face Erin and narrowed her gaze. As her mother's eyes raked over her hot red dress, Erin wondered if she had some telltale sign of a woman who'd recently had sex. No, not sex, she corrected herself. A woman who had recently made love.

"Erin, you might want to do something with your hair first."

Without warning, Kale stopped mid-stride and turned back to Erin. He dipped his head and touched her cheek. The longing in his eyes made her forget every sane thought. His fingers brushed against her flesh as he tucked a wayward lock behind her ear. His torrid, yearning gaze touched something deep inside her. Her knees began to quiver, and she became hyper aware of the moistness between her legs.

"There is nothing wrong with Erin's hair." A warm palm cupped her face. "She's beautiful just the way she is." His voice was smooth, low, and sent shivers skittering down her spine.

Oh God, he was going to kiss her. Right there in front of her mother and all her snooty guests, with their eagle eyes trained on the action. And she was going to let him. With no attempt at discretion, he brought his mouth to hers. Desire rocketed her over the goalpost as his lips crashed down on hers for a soul-searching kiss full of taunting promises.

In a bold move she wrapped her arms around Kale and kissed him in return, all the while ignoring her mother's small gasp of surprise. A moment later, Kale inched back. His smile was slow and inviting. He pitched his voice low and put his mouth near her ear. "I'll be back shortly. Remember where we were." His words wreaked havoc on her senses as his warm breath fanned her face, making her body quiver in the most delicious places.

After he moved away with her mother, Erin made a bee-line to the liquor cabinet and poured herself a stiff drink, hoping to quell the fever rising in her. She stood there, trying to remember how to breathe as she sucked back gin like it was soda pop. She cringed as it slid down her throat. The stuff was horrid.

Her sister Terry came up beside her. She rubbed her hands together like she were concocting some evil plan. All that was missing was the maniacal laughter. "Ooh, he's so hot. I just love him, Erin."

Oh God!

She was in trouble.

Because she loved him too.

Warmth sang through Erin's veins as she watched Kale mingle. Everything about him was so easy, so casual, and so comfortable. Every few minutes he'd glance her way and give her an intimate smile meant for her and her alone.

"He's so yummy, Erin."

Erin slanted her head to get a better look at her sister. Was that drool pooling in the corners of her mouth? Lord, the woman was married with kids. She shouldn't be salivating over Kale like Pavlov's dog. That was Erin's job.

"Where have you been hiding this fine specimen?" Terry asked.

Erin was far too preoccupied admiring Kale to answer her sister. His mere presence drew the attention of everyone at the party. All eyes were turned on him as he mingled with the guests. Erin watched him, her own body so in tune with his every gesture, his every movement.

Even though he was across the room, she felt so close to him. There was no denying she'd experienced an intimacy with him unlike anything she'd ever experienced before. And tonight, during their lovemaking, she knew she'd connected with him on a deeper level. Everything in her craved him. She needed to be with him. To touch him again and again, and to have him touch her in return.

Without answering her sister's question, she said, "I have to go, Terry."

As she moved across the floor toward him, her entire body began to quake. The minute she entered his personal space, the need to feel skin on skin, to connect with him on an even deeper level overwhelmed her. She didn't even fight the compulsion to wrap her arms around his waist, to find comfort in his embrace.

He pulled her in tight, glanced down at her, and smiled. Erin's insides turned to mush. "Are you okay?" he asked.

She wasn't okay. Not even a little bit. "Take me home, Kale."

His brow furrowed. "Home? To your place?"

It was late and she should go home, but she needed to be with him, to love him, and to make love to him while she could, while he was still in Iowa.

She shook her head. "No. Yours."

Chapter 11

Kale escorted Erin up the driveway to the front entrance. He opened the door, stepped inside, and hauled her in along with him. He felt her shiver as the cold seeped under her skin and penetrated her bones.

Kale rubbed his hands up and down her arms. "Are you cold?"

"A little."

He gave her a sexy grin. "I know the perfect way to heat you up."

"Yeah?"

"We never did get to try out that hot tub."

She chuckled. "Yes, I believe I was about to show you a fantasy or two of mine."

"Let's make it two," he teased.

They grabbed a couple of towels, stripped down to what

the good Lord gave them, and made their way to the patio doors. Erin's towel fell as she reached out and released the lock. She didn't bother covering herself back up. He loved that she was so uninhibited around him and so comfortable in her own skin.

"On the count of three we run," Erin said.

A cold gust of air rushed in. They both shivered.

"Forget that." Kale scooped her up, ran across the wooden deck, and deposited her in the water. He turned up the jets and jumped in beside her.

"Ahhhh, so nice," he said, moving closer.

They both rested their heads back and gazed at the stars twinkling in the dark night sky. Erin gave a contented sigh. "It's so beautiful out here."

Kale slanted his head sideways and stared at Erin. "Yes, so very beautiful."

She turned to him. Kale suspected she knew full well he was talking about her. He saw turmoil in her eyes and hoped he was getting to her. Hoped she was beginning to realize that what was between them went far beyond casual. Hoped she was learning to trust him and understand that he wasn't like other men in her life who'd destroyed her belief in happily-ever-after.

He wanted her so much it hurt. And wanted her to want him the same way. He knew instinctively, since the minute he'd set eyes on her, they were meant to be together. Forever.

He curled a strand of her damp hair through his fingers. "Now tell me about this fantasy of yours."

She puckered her lips and breathed a kiss over his cheek. "I don't think so."

"No?"

"No. I though I'd show you instead." She reached down and sheathed his cock in her hands. He pulsed and thickened as she squeezed her fingers around him.

A wide grin split his lips. "Well, if you must."

She chuckled. "Oh, I must."

She came around to kneel in front of him. One hand slid down to cradle his balls while the other stroked his cock. She leaned forward, pressed her lips lightly over his, and teased his cock between her breasts.

Lust settled deep in his groin as he became lost in the sensations. Closing his eyes, he threw his head back. "Oh, man, that's good."

"I want to taste you." Her sexy voice was breathy, intimate.

His head jerked up with a start. His gaze flew to her face. The women he'd been with in the past had always avoided that act for one reason or another. He brushed her hair back and looked deep into her eyes. "You would do that? For me?"

Her fingers marched over his stomach. "You got to taste me, now I want to taste you." Her eyes were dark and full of passion.

"Are you sure?"

Instead of answering, she rasped, "Lift your hips for me." Her hands circled around to grab his ass and lift him from

the water. "Oh, and Kale. It's for me too. It gives me pleasure to pleasure you." Her grin turned wicked as she lightly
brushed her tongue over her bottom lip.

He gulped.

Her smile prompted him into action. He planted his
elbows on the ceramic tub and raised his pelvis until the
night air kissed his swollen cock. The contrast of hot and
cold stimulated him, making his dick tighten and throb.

She held his cock in her hands and admired it. Her lips
parted as her eyes devoured him. "Very beautiful."

"Thanks," he croaked around the lump in his throat.
"Thanks" hardly seemed the appropriate response. It didn't
even begin to describe what he was feeling, what was in his
heart, and how happy she made him.

All thoughts were forgotten when she began massaging
his balls. She looked at him and breathed a kiss over his engorged phallus. "Now it's my turn to make you moan." With
a long, luxurious stroke she ran her tongue down the length
of him. She glanced at him, the devil's gleam in her eyes. "In
fact, I think I'll make you scream." She widened her mouth
to accommodate his thickness and drew him all the way to
the back of her throat.

He screamed all right. Moaned, growled, groaned, and
screamed.

Her cheeks curved inward as she sucked. Blood pounded
into his cock when her damp hair caressed his inner thighs.

With a feathery light caress, Erin worked her tongue over
his bulbous head while her hand stroked him in a smooth,

steady motion. His cock grew thicker as it absorbed the warmth of her mouth.

Erotic mewling sounds came from deep in her throat. He loved the sweet, sexy bedroom noises she made. Loved that she liked what she was doing. Balancing with one arm, Kale reached out and cupped her breasts, pinching her nipples between his fingers. She pushed against his hands and sucked harder. He drew in a tight breath as his body trembled and his pulse soared.

His liquid arousal pearled on the tip of his cock and Erin eagerly lapped it up. She licked her lips in sheer delight. "Mmmm. I love the taste of you, Kale."

That was enough to bring him to his breaking point. He clenched his jaw, unable to hold out any longer. Good Lord, he'd never come so fast in his life. "I'm going to come, babe." His voice was a strangled whisper.

"That's the plan," she teased. "I want you to come in my mouth, Kale."

Her words pushed him over the edge. He threw his head back and came on a growl. His liquid heat exploded into her hungry, waiting mouth.

After she swallowed every last drop, she lifted her head and met his glance. Smiling, she released a very satisfied sigh and licked his juices from her lips.

"Come closer," he said, tugging on her. She slid up his chest, her pert nipples brushing his skin, arousing him all over again. Kale drew her into his arms, captured her mouth, and swallowed her happy sigh.

He crushed his fingers through her hair. "I can't seem to get enough of you."

"Same here." She rested her head against his chest and drew a contented breath.

"Well, I can hardly blame you, Erin." He puffed out his chest. "I *am* magnificent."

Erin chuckled. She lifted her head, rolled her eyes, and splashed water in his face. "Yes, I'm sure that must be the reason."

As he cupped her chin and drew her lips to his, her stomach growled. His quickly joined the chorus. As they shared a private chuckle, Kale brushed her damp hair from her forehead.

"Why don't we take the shrimp back to bed and eat it there?"

A sparkle twinkled in her eyes and her lips turned up naughtily. "The sauce too?"

His heart swelled in his chest. God, he was so crazy about her, and now that they'd advanced their relationship to the next stage, Kale had every intention of pushing her further.

Kale gathered her in his arms and hugged her. "You are such a bad girl. Come on." He jumped from the tub and knotted a towel around his waist. He held hers out for her and pulled it tight around her shoulders after she climbed out of the water. Hand in hand, they bolted inside.

Erin briskly rubbed her arms. "Brrrr."

"Let's go get under the covers and warm up." Kale grabbed the shrimp and sauce from the fridge. Keeping pace, he followed Erin down the hall. She pushed open the door and stepped inside the bedroom. The scent of their earlier love-making perfumed the air and spilled into the hall.

Erin dropped her towel, got on her hands and knees, and crawled across the mattress. Kale gulped air. His cock surged to life in reaction to the erotic sight before him. He wasn't kidding when he said he couldn't get enough of her. She was more potent and addictive than any sex drug designed at the lab. He placed the shrimp platter on the nightstand. At that moment he had other things besides food occupying his mind.

"Um, Erin. Stay exactly like that."

"What?" She smiled at him over her shoulder.

He cleared his throat, pinched the knot on his towel, and let it fall to the floor. Her gaze followed it, then lifted back to lock with his. "I just remembered another one of my fantasies." He ran his hand over her rounded backside and squeezed her tender flesh.

Her smile faded. A stricken look came over her. She lowered her lashes, shadowing her emotions. "I … uh …" She faltered and twisted around until she was sitting on the edge of the bed. Her feet tangled together, her hands clasping tightly.

Kale sat on the bed beside her and finger combed her hair. He slanted his head and gazed deep into her turbulent eyes. "What is it?"

Her mouth curved downward. "Not like that, okay?"

He matched her frown. "Are you sore?"

She shook her head no.

He tucked a damp strand behind her ears. "Does this position hurt you? Erin, I'd never want to do anything to hurt you."

Her eyes softened, and he could see she appreciated his concern. "No, it's not that."

"Come here, babe." He gathered her into his embrace and stroked his hands over her arms. "What is it then?"

When she didn't answer, he pressed. "Talk to me, Erin. Tell me what's wrong." He wanted her to trust him, to open up to him.

"It's silly, really." He could tell she was uncomfortable and wanted to comfort her.

"Of course it's not silly, Erin. If it's important to you, then it's important to me."

She reached out and absentmindedly curled his wet hair through her fingers. "I was engaged a few years ago."

His back stiffened in surprise. "Really?" His brow furrowed as a surge of jealousy tugged on his emotions. "I didn't realize that."

"I came home from work early one day and found my ex screwing his secretary on my bed in that same position. I guess it just brings back painful memories from my past."

He tightened his grip around her, offering his comfort, his understanding. "Asshole," he mumbled under his breath.

She nodded her head. "Yeah, he was. I'm glad I found out what kind of guy he was before I married him."

He paused and considered the situation. Now he finally

understood why she was so guarded. "This actually explains a lot."

She furrowed her brow. "What do you mean?"

He touched her cheek, stroking his finger over her tender skin. She leaned into him, accepting his warmth. "There had to be a reason you felt men were good for sex and nothing more. You were hurt, Erin. That's understandable."

She rested her head against his chest and heaved a sigh. "You know, Kale, I was young, naïve, and in love with the idea of being in love. I had always wanted a family and jumped at the first guy who asked me to marry him. My mother pressuring me didn't help either. I could have made the biggest mistake of my life."

"I want you to point this asshole out to me next time you see him."

She lifted her head and met his glance. "You do?"

"Yeah, after I punch him in the mouth, I'd like to thank him."

"Thank him?"

"Thank him for being an asshole because if he wasn't, then I would have missed out on this." Cupping her chin, he lifted her mouth to his and brushed his lips over hers for a warm, tender kiss.

She smiled and put her hand over his as it caressed her face.

Kale inched back. "Why are you smiling?"

"I'm going to thank him too."

Pleasure Prolonged

Kale's heart turned over in his chest. "Let's lie down." He eased her back until she was nestled against her pillow. He snuggled in beside her and held her close. She wiggled in his arms, trying to get closer. A comfortable silence fell over them as they held on to each other for a long, quiet moment. Her breathing deepened, and he sensed she was on the brink of sleep.

Kale pulled the blankets over them. "Let's get some rest, sweetheart," he whispered.

"Kale?" Her voice was feathery soft, drowsy.

"Yeah?"

"When do you leave?"

"In a month."

"Okay."

"I might stay longer, though."

"Really?"

"Yeah."

"Why?"

"I like my job here." He kissed her forehead and pulled her impossibly closer. "With the right incentive, I'd like to make my stay permanent."

Many hours later Erin awoke. She peeled her eyes open and glanced at the window. The winter sun, low on the horizon, began its early morning ascent and glistened on the window-pane. She blinked and twisted sideways to see the clock. It was still very early. Fortunately, they didn't have to be at work for hours. That would give her plenty of time to pull to-gether the plan she'd gone over a hundred times in her mind before she drifted off to sleep last night.

Kale was sound asleep, snoring lightly beside her. She gazed at the light dusting of stubble shadowing his jaw and admitted to herself how much he'd come to mean to her and how much she loved him. So much for her plan to have casual sex and not fall for him. She had been crazy to think she could separate herself from her emotions. Kale's tender touch had penetrated her defenses. Not to mention the thoughtful way he treated her.

When he smiled in his sleep, emotions so powerful that they left her shaken coursed through her body. Warmth settled in her stomach. Honestly, how could she not fall in love with a guy who put her feelings, career, and well-being first? A guy whose lovemaking was so full of warmth, emo-tion, and tenderness? A loyal, responsible guy who loved and cared for his family?

She swept her gaze down the length of his magnificent, naked body. A prickle of awareness washed over her as she slowly perused him. Skating her tongue over her lips, she took a fortifying breath and carefully pulled his blankets over him, resisting the urge to brush his hair from his fore-head for fear of waking him.

He mumbled something in his sleep and twisted side-ways, pulling the blankets with him.

She knew she had told him this relationship was casual and nothing more, but she had quickly learned there was nothing casual about Kale. When it came to her needs and desires, he was thoughtful, caring, and compassionate. He'd made her rethink what she wanted out of life. Taught her to put the past behind her and move on with the future, because not all guys were insensitive assholes like Dwayne. Trust didn't come easily to her, yet deep inside her, she instinctively trusted him and knew he'd never do anything to hurt her. Loving him felt so right, so natural.

He said he wanted to stick around for his job. This morning, if things went according to her well-thought-out plan, she planned on giving him another incentive to stick around.

She drew a deep, calming breath, climbed from the bed, and went in search of her clothes. After she quickly dressed, she jotted her address down on a slip of paper and placed it on her pillow.

It was time to muster her courage, take a chance on love, and let him know that in her quest to be a bad girl she'd developed more than casual feelings for him, and pray that he returned those feelings.

Chapter *12*

Kale's hands automatically reached beside him as the alarm clock pulled him from his sleep. When his fingers came up empty, he jolted upright. Fuck! He glanced around the room. Erin's clothes were gone. His gut sank. Damn, she must have slipped out while he slept. His mind raced with the turn of events. Did her running out mean she had no intention of letting this relationship evolve beyond casual?

He spotted the slip of paper beside him. Hope rushed through him as he picked it up and read it. The words *see you again, breakfast,* and *my place* were all he needed to read to prompt him into action. He was on his feet and showering in less than a minute. After dressing hastily, he was out the door and in his truck.

Less than a half hour later he was standing outside Erin's

condo door. He prayed she wasn't trying to let him down easy over a plate of eggs.

He lifted his hand to knock. Erin swung the door open before he had a chance.

"You came," she blurted and then blew out what appeared to be a relieved breath, as though she had been worried he wouldn't show. Her brown eyes lit with excitement as she reached for him.

He was thrilled at how excited she was to see him. He too blew out a breath and relaxed as he perused her. She was dressed in a light gray jogging suit that hugged her curves in all the right places. Her hair was damp from a recent shower. His heart lurched at the sight of her. The love he felt for her came over him, making him slightly dizzy. He exhaled and tugged at his collar.

"I came."

She grinned and pulled him inside. "Yes, you have. And you will again and again," she teased, throwing his words back at him.

He chuckled, then wrapped his hands around her waist. His voice turned serious. "I didn't like waking up without you beside me."

She gave him an apologetic look. "I wanted to make you breakfast."

He lowered his head and kissed her, his hands touching her all over, yet unable to get enough of her. "You wanted to cook for me?"

She pursed her lips. "Yeah, I'm a closet domestic," she admitted.

He smiled. "But you could have done that at my place."

She matched him kiss for kiss and touch for touch. It thrilled and exhilarated him how responsive she was. "I wanted to do it here." She waved her hand through the air. "In my place."

Was she saying what he thought she was saying? Was she welcoming him into more than just her home? Had she finally realized that what was between them wasn't casual? Had she learned to put the past behind her and allow herself to love again?

"I see." Love rushed to his heart when she smiled at him. His entire being, body and soul, reached out to her.

"Follow me." She grabbed his hand, led him into the kitchen, and motioned for him to take a seat at her small dinette table.

Kale knew it was well past time to tell her how he felt. It was time to move past the casual sex games. To lay his heart on the line and see if she felt the same way.

He lowered his voice. "Erin, I think we need to talk."

With the spatula in her hand, she turned around to face him. She nodded in agreement. "You're right." She dropped the spatula, turned off the stove, and took a seat beside him. "I have something to tell you."

"You do?"

"Yes." She leaned forward and planted her arms on the table. She blew out a breath and rushed on. "I'm not a bad girl," she blurted out. "I'm a fake, a fraud. I talk tough and pretend I'm experienced, but I'm not really." She threw her hands in the air and continued to ramble uncensored. "I was pretending to be something I wasn't. I wanted to put my money where my mouth was, well not quite, but I think you know what I mean, and see what it was like to have a casual affair."

"I know."

Her eyes flew open. Her head jerked back with a start. "You do?"

"Of course I do."

"But," she stammered. "How?"

He touched her chin. "Sweetheart, I knew from the minute I looked into your expressive eyes, you were all talk and no action. That you weren't into casual sex." He inched closer, his heart picking up tempo. "Why are you telling me this?" He held his breath, hoping, praying she was ready to give their love a chance.

"I know we agreed to keep things casual." She paused and toyed with the tablecloth. "And I thought I could." She glanced up at him, her eyes serious. "But I was wrong."

His heart nearly burst through his chest as her words touched him in a way he'd never been touched before. He exhaled with relief and joy.

He felt as if a huge weight had been lifted from his shoulders. He angled his head and met her gaze. "I never agreed to keep it casual."

Thick black lashes fluttered over dark eyes. "You didn't?" Her breath seemed to catch in her throat.

He grinned. "Nope, not once. I knew from the minute I met you it could never be casual between us."

"But I thought you said—"

He cut her off. "I never said I wanted it to be casual." He reached out and closed his hands over hers. "And I don't want it to be casual, Erin. I want more out of this relationship."

She brushed her fingers over his jaw. "Why didn't you tell me?"

"You weren't ready to hear it. I needed to prove to you that I could be someone you could trust, and show you I wouldn't hurt you."

She nodded in understanding.

"I'm crazy about you, Erin."

The happiness in her expression warmed him all over. She jumped up and wrapped her arms around his neck. Her eyes were watery, her cheeks a darker shade of pink. "I'm crazy about you too, Kale." Her voice was tangled with love and emotion.

He held her tight and squeezed, never wanting to let go. "You have no idea how happy I am to hear that." He furrowed his brow. "When I woke up this morning I thought I'd lost you. I don't ever want to feel that way again." A frown pulled down the corners of his mouth.

"You won't," she assured him.

He pulled her onto his lap and gazed deep into her eyes. "I don't just want you in my bedroom, sweetheart. I want you in my life. I want to have a family with you."

Her smile widened. "I want you in my life too, Kale. I want you to stay here in Iowa, with me."

"I plan on it."

"You do?"

He nodded.

She angled her head and narrowed her eyes in mock annoyance. "And you neglected to tell me that, why?"

He chuckled. "Because I wanted you to ask me to stay. I wanted it to matter to you. I wanted you to want me in your life."

Erin's grin turned wicked. "I want you in my life, Kale, but right now I *really* want you in my bedroom." She stood up and held her hand out to him.

Kale jumped to his feet and wrapped his arms around her. "That would be my pleasure," he said.

Before they rounded the corner to the bedroom, the doorbell rang. Erin crinkled her nose and glanced at the clock.

"Are you expecting company?" Kale asked.

"No." Frowning, Erin hastily padded to the door, pulled it open, and came face-to-face with Deanne. Hooker Barbie's plastic grin deepened Erin's frown.

"What do you want?" Erin asked. Kale moved in beside Erin and wrapped his arm around her waist in a protective manner.

Ignoring her question, Deanne turned to Kale. "Kale, you naughty boy. Did you go through my locker last night? You know that wasn't part of *our* plan."

"What do you want, Deanne?" he asked.

Her expression turned serious. "The game is over, Kale." Deanne glared at Erin. "Kale was in on it with me all along. We both wanted to work together and get you out of the picture." Her gaze raced over Erin. "Apparently he's been doing a little slumming while he was at it."

Kale fisted his hands. "That's bullshit and you know it."

Deanne scoffed. "You can stop pretending now, Kale." She shot Erin a wry grin and rolled her eyes. "You know you can't believe anything coming out of the mouth of a playboy. He'll tell you anything to get you into his bed." She gave Erin a once-over. "It appears Kale has already told you what you wanted to hear to get you between the sheets." Deanne held out a computer disk. "This will prove it to you, Erin. Watch this and you'll see that Kale and I have been working together and we too had a little fun in the research room. You're not the only one he's ... fucking, in more ways than one."

Kale swallowed as anger rushed through him. Jesus H. Christ. He turned to Erin. Her face was white, her eyes wide.

"Erin, it's not what you think."

He reached for her but she faltered backward. "It's not?" she asked, her brow furrowing.

His heart beat in a mad cadence. Fuck, he couldn't lose her now. Not after they'd laid everything on the line. He gripped her shoulders. "No. It's not."

Erin gave a tight nod. "Then why don't I tell you what

I think, and you can see if I'm right or not." She turned to face Deanne. "I think Deanne's pretty pissed that she didn't get my job, and I think she would go to great lengths to get me fired or try to hurt me." Erin grabbed the disk from her hand and tossed it onto her side table. "I don't need to see this. I already know what's on there, and I also know things aren't always as they seem." Erin stepped closer to Deanne, urging her back outside. With that she slammed the door and turned back to face Kale.

Incredulous, he stood there slack jawed. The love he felt for her overwhelmed him, making it nearly impossible to draw air. "Thank you for having faith in me and believing in us." He picked her up and spun her around. "God, I love you so much, Erin."

She squeezed him back. "Oh, Kale, I love you too," she echoed. Her eyes suddenly turned serious. "What are we going to do about Deanne?" Erin asked.

"Now that I'm leaving Castech, I believe there is going to be a job opening. I'll be able to get her a transfer."

"Really, why would you do that for her?"

"I'm doing it for us. We don't need her causing any more trouble around the office. Besides, she'll fit in there perfectly."

Erin offered him a smile. "Great idea." She grabbed Kale's hand. "Now that that's been taken care of, come with me. I have more important matters on my mind. I want to make love with you."

Cathryn Fox

She ushered him into the bedroom, both tearing their clothes away as they went. "Shit, Erin. I didn't bring any condoms."

"That's okay, we don't need any."

"We don't?"

She turned back to face him. A grin curled her beautiful mouth. "You said you wanted to have a family with me, didn't you?"

He grabbed her and kissed her with all the love inside him. She melted against him and matched the intensity of his kiss.

She inched away and climbed onto her bed, where she positioned herself on her hands and knees. "I want you to make love to me, like this," she murmured.

His heart tightened. He reached for her, pulled her to her feet, and drew her to him. "Erin, no. You don't have to do that. Not like this. Not for me." Her gesture touched him in places so deep, he thought his heart would burst.

"Don't you see, it's for me, Kale." She covered his cheek with her palm. "I don't want to hold on to old, painful memories. I want to make new memories. Here on my bed with you. I trust you and it's what I truly want."

He hesitated, deliberating on what to do. "Are you sure, babe?"

She nodded.

He touched her cheek and feathered his fingers over her lips. His gaze searched her eyes for answers. Suddenly, understanding dawned on him. He pitched his voice low as his heart turned over in his chest. He found it most difficult to speak. "You're wrong, Erin. This isn't just for you or just for me. It's a gift, for both of us."

Her gaze was direct, unwavering. "Yes, Kale, it's a gift, for both of us. I want this, and you, more than anything." She reached down and stroked his cock, her hands tightening and loosening as her fingers glided up and down the long length of him. He throbbed as blood pumped into his veins. "I believe you want this too." The devil's grin curled her lips.

He slapped her ass and shook his head. "You're so naughty." His hand circled around to her silky curls. He dipped a finger between her folds. Her liquid heat flooded his fingers. "Mmmmmm. I love that you're always so wet for me." She moaned and wiggled, driving his finger in deeper.

"You have magical fingers, Kale." She pushed her pelvis against him, massaging his rock-hard erection with her hip. "Now show me what you can do with *that*." Her voice was low, coaxing.

Backing away, she flicked her hair over her shoulders and climbed onto her hands and knees. She jiggled her ass back and forth, teasing him, urging him on.

Kale stared wide-eyed at the gorgeous, sexy woman posed before him. He barely remembered how to breathe. Her damp sex glistened from her arousal. He was anxious to make sweet love to her, but first, he had to have a small sampling.

"I'll show you what I can do after I taste you." The edge of the bed dipped as he leaned forward and inhaled her rich, sensual scent. He parted her pretty pink lips and hungrily licked her creamy essence, his thumb climbing higher to stroke her clitoris.

Her body vibrated and convulsed. "Oh my." Her voice was intimate, breathy. "You have a magical tongue too."

Kale stood back up, gripped her hips, and pulled her closer to the edge. He rubbed the tip of his cock between her fleshy lips, purposely nudging her swollen clitoris, teasing the sensitive nerve endings. His bulbous head breached her opening when she bucked against him and cried out his name.

With one quick plunge he entered her. The instant bond of intimacy made his heart swell in his chest. She drew a sharp breath as her muscles spasmed around him. Her heat closed over his cock like a warm glove. It felt so damn good to be inside her, no latex barrier separating their flesh.

With needy, urgent thrusts, he rammed into her. She shifted, driving him in deeper. In no time at all he felt her hot release of pressure.

"Oh, Kale, I'm there."

Feeling his own orgasm mounting, he leaned forward and stroked her breasts. He took quick panting breaths. "I love you so much, Erin. Thank you for loving me, and trusting me, and wanting to make new memories with me."

"I ... love ... you ... too." She ended on a moan as he pumped his semen into her.

Erin twisted around and collapsed onto her back. She reached for him. He climbed into the bed beside her and drew the covers over them.

She looked deep into his eyes and snuggled into him as though unable to get close enough. The love on her face took his breath away. "I believe we'll have to do it like this more often."

"You know, Erin, deep down inside you exists a very naughty, very bad girl."

Her laugh was throaty, sexy. "I know, Kale. It just took the right bad boy to unleash her."

Sitting in the passenger seat of Kale's truck, Erin studied his handsome profile as he pulled into his parking space at Iowa Research Center. He must have sensed her gaze on him. He shot her a sidelong glance and smiled. She could see the love he felt for her shining in his eyes.

He reached out and squeezed her hand. "We're late," he said.

She grinned and stifled a yawn. "Sam is going to have a fit but he'll cover for us. He's a great guy."

They climbed from the truck and rushed inside the building. By the time they stepped into the lobby, Sam was pacing back and forth, Rio clinging to his side.

"Where have you two been? I didn't know how much longer I could cover for you." He took a look at them both and said, "Never mind. I don't think I want to know. Come on, your test subjects are waiting."

They all climbed into the waiting elevator. Kale glanced at the number pad, then exchanged a look with Erin. In unison they both glanced at Sam, giving him a look that suggested he might want to wait for the next elevator.

He was quick to catch on. With determined strides, he stepped back into the lobby. Rolling his eyes, he darted his gaze back and forth between the two of them. "I ... uh ... think I'll catch the next one. Before you two corrupt me." He put his hands over his chimp's eyes. "And Rio."

He winked at Erin and gave an approving shake of his head as the metal doors slammed shut.

"I like him," Kale said.

"I like him too," she agreed. "But I like you a lot more."

A bad-boy grin curled his mouth. He reached out and pulled her into his arms. "Show me."

Erin unzipped his pants and proceeded to do just that!

Chapter 13

Erin glanced up from her notes as Kale lowered himself onto the stool beside her. His warmth and love reached out to her as he tucked a wayward strand of hair behind her ear. Her body trembled with need as his warm fingers grazed her skin. That small gesture always turned her inside out.

She angled her head and smiled. Her gaze panned his face as she leaned into him. God, he was so handsome. She closed her eyes for a brief moment, inhaling, letting his scent curl around her.

Needing to touch him, to feel a connection, she put her hand on his cheek. It still baffled her that a little over a week ago, she'd vowed to keep things casual. Now here she was totally in love with Kale and planning a spring wedding. Her other hand automatically moved to her stomach. She'd once heard a woman say she knew the minute she'd become pregnant. Erin had been skeptical of such a claim, until now. She knew deep in her soul that during their lovemaking they had made a beautiful baby. Her heart filled with hope and joy. She just knew Kale would be an amazing father.

"Hey," she said.

"Hey yourself." His passion-imbued eyes kicked her pulse into high gear.

She drew a fortifying breath. "Are you ready?" she asked, closing her notebook.

"You bet."

Earlier that morning they'd presented their data to the director, and now they were anxiously waiting for him to call a meeting, to inform them whether their experiment was ready to be presented to the grant governing board or whether more testing needed to be performed.

Sam pushed open the security door. "Hey you two, the director is ready to see you."

Erin's heart fluttered, her pulse beat in a mad cadence. Her gaze darted from the door to Kale. "We have to tell him about us, you know."

Kale stood and pulled her up along with him. Her body collided with his. "I know. I'll tell him," Kale said easily.

Erin crinkled her nose. "He frowns on office affairs, and I don't want this to interfere with my promotion."

Kale rolled his shoulder. "Then we have nothing to worry about," he assured her. He dropped a tender kiss onto her forehead. "Because we're not having an office affair. I love you, and I want to marry you."

Erin smiled. She would never tire of hearing him say that.

Kale clasped her hand in his. "Let's go."

A few minutes later Erin found herself sitting across from the director as he perused the open file on his desk. She tried to assess him, but his expression remained masked.

He slowly closed the file. His glance went from Kale, to Erin, back to Kale again. He narrowed his gaze. "I received an unexpected request from Deanne today. She put in for a transfer to Castech, based on your recommendation, Kale."

Kale nodded. "Now that I'm staying here permanently, a junior researcher will undoubtedly move up into my position and there will be a hole to fill. I think she'll fit in perfectly," Kale assured him.

He raised an eyebrow. "I wonder what could have happened around the lab while I was gone. The last I knew Deanne was happy working here."

Kale shrugged, offering no explanation.

Reginald planted his hands on his desk. "Okay, enough about Deanne. I'm sure you two are anxious to hear about the experiment."

Erin nodded eagerly.

He waved his hand over the file before him. "The data you both compiled clearly indicate the success of the serum. I believe the grant governing board will be quite thrilled with the results. I'll make arrangements for you to present next week."

Erin clapped her hands together. "Fantastic."

"Good job, you two. I'm impressed with hard work and dedication. Erin, you'll make a fine wing supervisor."

Kale grabbed her hand and squeezed, offering silent congratulations.

The director stood. "Now, if that is all, you two can take the rest of the day off. You deserve it."

Erin shot a nervous glance at Kale.

"Actually there is one more thing," Kale said.

The director reclaimed his chair and arched an inquisitive brow. "Go on."

Kale squeezed Erin's hand more tightly and spoke with confidence. "I'm in love with Erin and we're getting married."

The director didn't even seem fazed. He leaned back in his chair and folded his arms across his chest. "Really? That didn't take long."

Taken aback by his comment, Erin's head jerked back. "What?" she asked, confused by his reaction.

Reginald rocked in his seat. "That was much quicker than we would have suspected."

Erin stood and stammered over her words. "What do you mean?"

"I mean Laura and Jay fully expected you two to fall in love. It's just that none of us thought it would happen so fast." He chuckled. "And of course when Laura asked me to duly warn you both about stepping out of line at the office, she knew it would succeed in driving you together faster. She said deep down you were a bit of a rebel, Erin."

"Ohmigod," Erin blurted as realization dawned. The three of them had been matchmaking.

Reginald narrowed his gaze. "Erin, are you feeling okay? You look a little flushed."

"I just ... I just ..."

Laughing, Kale stood and gathered her into his arms. "I think Jay knew how I felt about you from the first minute I set eyes on you."

He hugged her tighter and Erin melted into him. She lifted her gaze to his. "And obviously Laura knew how I felt about you too."

A broad smile stretched across his face, the director piped in, "We all knew. Heck, everyone at the wedding knew." He waved a dismissive hand. "Now go on. Go celebrate your success and your love and do what young people do."

Erin and Kale both turned to leave. "Oh, and one more thing." The director's words stopped them mid-stride. They both turned back.

He angled his head and put on his best stern face. "Please keep your home videos where they belong. In your home."

Mortified, Erin's hand flew to her mouth. She felt color bloom high on her cheeks. "Ohmigod, how—"

Reginald shook his head. "It's my job to know everything that goes on here." He stood and moved around to the other side of the desk. "Now go. You have a celebration to attend and a wedding to plan." He waved his hand. "And do try to stay out of trouble," he added with a wink.

Epilogue

Epilogue

Six months later

The knock on the door was a welcome distraction from the endless packing. God, who knew she had so much junk. Erin stood and padded softly across her small living room. Warm summer sunshine spilled inside the entrance as she swung open the door.

"Since when did you start knocking?" She stepped back and motioned for Sam to enter.

He grinned and nodded toward Kale. "Since you married him."

"Hey, Sam," Kale called out. "You're here just in time to help me load the truck."

Erin turned back to Kale and smiled. She loved how her two favorite guys had become such good buddies. She would miss Sam's daily visits when she moved across town. But now that they were married, they definitely needed a bigger place. And after the success of Pleasure Prolonged, and both their advancements, they could now afford her dream house in the burbs.

"I really hate that you're moving, you know." He touched his hand to her stomach. "Now I won't get to see the little guy every day."

Erin's heart softened. "Or the little girl," she corrected. "And of course you can see little Sam any time you want." She winked at him.

"Sam?" he said.

"Yeah, it's a great name for a boy or a girl, don't you think?"

Surprised registered on his face. He blinked. "Really?"

Erin chuckled. "Yes, really. Kale and I want to name the baby after you."

Sam put his hand over his heart. "Thank you, Erin. This means so much to me. It's an honor." Suddenly a frown crossed his face. "But I still don't want you to move so far. When will I see little Sam?"

"I believe as godfather you have special privileges that allow you to visit any time you want." She motioned for him to grab a chair before turning her attention to Kale. "Should we tell him?"

Kale carried a box to the door, dropped it, then came back to stand beside her. "He looks like he needs something to cheer him up."

"Tell me what?" Sam asked, his blue eyes sparkling with renewed interest.

"Well, Kale and I had a conference with the director yesterday. And since Kale is going to take leave to stay home with me for the first couple of months, we're going to need someone to oversee the Pleasure Exchange experiment in our absence."

Sam's mouth dropped open. "Are you saying what I think you're saying?"

Erin could barely contain her excitement. "Yup, you get the lead. You're getting your own lab and your own team."

Sam jumped up. "Really?"

"Congratulations, Sam," Kale said, patting him on the shoulder.

"You'll be testing a female libido enhancer," Erin added.

The corner of his mouth lifted as he wrapped his arms around Erin's waist and swung her in the air. "Hot damn."

Kale furrowed his brows. "Hey, watch my baby." He put a protective arm around Erin and pulled her close.

Erin rolled her eyes. Now that she was pregnant, he doted on her every need and treated her like a china doll. But she loved every minute of it.

Sam laughed and stepped back. "This is fantastic news."

Kale nudged him. "Just think about how much fun you're going to have testing that one."

Erin chuckled. "I know at least a dozen women around the lab who'd be anxious to sign on as your test subject."

And maybe, Erin thought, maybe he'd find love during his experiment the same way she had.

Following is a sneak peek at
Cathryn Fox's newest erotic novel . . .
the third in the Pleasure Games series

PLEASURE EXCHANGE

And here she thought things couldn't get any worse.

Surrounded by rowdy animal rights activists, journalist Cathleen Nichols rolled her eyes heavenward and wondered who the hell she'd pissed off in a past lifetime to deserve this. As if standing on a picket line outside the Iowa Research Center in a deluge of cold autumn rain with her makeup smeared and her hair plastered to her forehead wasn't enough to top off a perfectly shitty day, she'd spotted *him*.

The man who despised her.

The man who'd be thrilled to see her in such a predicament.

The same man who'd been starring in her fantasies for the past six months.

Oh hell.

Who knew the article she'd written about the Iowa Research Center's sexual experiments would draw so much attention? Negative attention, that is.

For him.

From behind the lobby doors, his piercing blue eyes sifted through the crowd and settled on her. *Oh boy!* Desire thrummed through her veins as their gazes collided. On her date rating scale this man scored a triple A. Anywhere, anytime, anything . . .

She'd been living across the courtyard from not-so-nerdy scientist Sam York for a little more than six months. Except for the day he'd helped her carry in packing boxes, they'd barely spoken. She'd come to learn he dedicated his spare time to his work and didn't have much room in his life for other luxuries.

Luxuries like having her writhing beneath him on his king-sized bed. Her pulse leaped into action as she played out that provocative image. *Cripes! This wasn't the time to indulge in her rich sexual fantasies.*

She'd also come to learn that he spent many evenings at home, alone with his pet chimpanzee, Rio, poring over research. And after a long, tiring night of work, he'd sometimes forget to close his blinds when he undressed for bed.

Not that she watched and waited.

Not at all.

Not much anyway.

Her body fairly vibrated as she mentally indulged in the erotic slide show. Sexual longing swamped her, liquid heat moistening the juncture between her legs. She swallowed, her throat suddenly the only dry part of her body.

Even though they were neighbors, they seldom crossed paths. On those rare occasions when they bumped into each other outside the building, they'd exchanged pleasantries. The soft warmth of his voice always pulled at her as his rich scent singed her blood and sent heat curling through her veins.

Sam usually left the house minutes before her, but never failed to leave behind his spicy masculine aroma. It permeated the courtyard and seduced her senses. Cat inhaled, clinging to the enticing memory.

The restless crowd grew louder as they chanted and walked in circles around her. Camera crews milled about, filming the action for the evening news. Shaken from her fantasies, Cat glanced up to see Sam push past the lobby doors and step outside. Even though his mouth was set in a grim line, his captivating eyes still glimmered with dark sensuality.

With determined strides, Sam stalked forward. High over his head, his black umbrella bobbed like a buoy in the sea of people. More rankled than a caged animal, he weaved his way through the congestion and advanced toward her.

Shit!

Cat glanced at the clouds knitting together in the ominous, late afternoon sky. Where the hell was a bolt of lightning when she needed it?

A protester's threatening voice boomed from behind. "Hey buddy, you're not going to get away with this. I'll personally see to it that you never experiment on that chimp of yours again."

Lord, she'd barely mentioned the chimp in the article, yet activists had jumped all over that minor point, turning the parking lot into a circus sideshow.

Cat scanned the crowd and noted with mute interest how the majority of women seemed more enamored with Sam than annoyed. Eyes full of lust, they swarmed him, touching him with intimate recognition as he passed. They looked like a bevy of sharks ready to launch into a feeding frenzy. Cat snorted, suddenly annoyed. She knew exactly what those predators were interested in feasting on. It wasn't as if she could blame them, really. When Sam's smoldering baby blues turned on her, it made her want to drop her panties too.

The loud male protester moved in beside her and continued his rant. His voice vibrated right through Cat, eliciting a shudder from deep within. Cat pressed her palms to her ears to block out the ungodly sound. She had one nerve left and the man was riding it.

She twisted sideways to glimpse the protester, who was as relentless as a pit bull and louder than a gaggle of preteens beheading a piñata. Well hell! Recognition hit like a high-voltage jolt. It was none other than Eugene Letterman, a man who showed up at every protest, regardless of the cause.

As the camera turned on him, she cursed under her breath and tried not to feel as flustered as she felt. She looked heavenward. "Great. Kill me now." Cat linked her fingers together before she did something she'd regret. Like inflict bodily harm on the infamous protester.

Eugene Letterman. Otherwise known as Mr. Glory Hound around her office. An unemployed movie-star wannabe working on turning his fifteen minutes of fame into a career.

Cat cringed as he spouted rude comments and made obscene gestures with his freakishly long middle finger. Cripes, his remarks were making this situation so much worse for Sam. Surely one little jab in the ribs wouldn't get her into too much trouble. The sudden, delightful image of Eugene dangling from a tree and Cat with a foot-long stick rushed through her mind. The visual made her grin.

She turned back to face Sam as he approached. A scowl etched his handsome face as he pinned her with a glare. Her smile dropped out of sight faster than Eugene Letterman after the cameras turned off. Starching her spine, she rooted her feet, jerked her chin up, and steeled herself. The look in Sam's eyes told her this was not going to be one of their pleasant courtyard exchanges.

It hadn't been her intention to piss Sam off or rattle animal rights activists. All she had wanted was to pen an article that would make her editor, Blain Grant, stand up and take notice of her writing skills. If she couldn't branch out and prove to Blain that she had the talent to write serious pieces, no New York publishers would ever consider hiring her, and she'd never become a successful journalist like her father.

Her heart softened as she thought of her parents. It had

been their dream to see their only daughter follow in her father's footsteps. The motor vehicle accident that had left her and her six older brothers parentless two years previous had acted as a catalyst for Cat, driving her to strive harder to move beyond tongue-in-cheek fluff articles to serious, hard-hitting news.

Just last week the ideal job had opened at the *Daily Press* in New York. In her quest to write journalistic pieces, she'd forwarded her résumé along with a copy of her Iowa research article, the same article that had Sam riled. But without any other substantial experience or noteworthy news stories under her belt, she seriously doubted they'd give her a second glance, especially in such a fiercely competitive market.

Her editor gave all the hard-hitting news to Eric Hawkins, otherwise know as Hawk. Cat preferred to think he'd derived the nickname from his long pointed nose and beady eyes rather than his "Eye of the Hawk" column.

Cat's attention returned to Sam as he cut a path through the crowd. She quickly palmed her hair and smoothed it from her face. Cat didn't know why she was so concerned about her appearance. Why bother trying to make herself look presentable for Sam York? He probably hated her, and honestly, she really didn't care how she looked to him.

Not at all.

Not much anyway.

Hell, who was she kidding? She wanted Sam. Upside down, inside out, but mostly on top. Perhaps it was her lack of dating or her inability to attract a decent guy that had her libido in an uproar and her mind conjuring up fantasies about her neighbor.

In truth, the downtown dating scene had left her colder than a snowman's balls. It hadn't taken her long to figure out she was a jackass magnet.

Cat wasn't looking for true love or any type of long-term relationship. After all, she had a career to concentrate on and was counting down the days until she could move to New York. The last thing she wanted was a man to keep her tied in Iowa, preventing her from reaching her goal. She'd seen too many of her friends have babies and give up careers for a man, only to end up broken and unhappy. That wasn't going to happen to her.

Nope, no way, not her. She hadn't spent years in journalism school to toss all that education out the window because some man gave her a panty-soaking smile, or to write fluff articles for a small-time press, no matter how much she enjoyed it. With fierce determination, Cat had set her sights on *bigger and better*, as her father had always posed it. She planned on moving to New York, where she could write articles that mattered. Articles that had value.

In the interim, however, a date or two with a nice guy would certainly be a welcome distraction. Unfortunately, she couldn't meet a nice guy if her life depended on it. Well, that wasn't entirely true. She'd met Sam York. And he certainly seemed nice enough. On many occasions, she'd watched him carry in groceries and hold the door for the elderly tenants in their complex. Call her old-fashioned, but she liked it when a man showed a little chivalry. Small, thoughtful gestures went a long way in her book.

Underneath his nerdy lab coat existed one hell of a sexy guy. Too bad he had more interest in his work and his chimp than in her. And how did she remedy that small inconvenient problem? By writing an article on him and the lab's sexual experiments. Now he was lavishing her with lots of attention. Just not the kind she'd envisioned.

Brilliant!

Totally freaking brilliant!

The one man she wanted to get naked with didn't want to get naked with her.

She let out a long sigh.

Wasn't life a bitch like that?

The crowd tightened and moved forward as Sam stalked toward her. His eyes flared as they met hers. Shutting out the din of the protesters, she narrowed her focus and concentrated all her attention on Mr. Sexy Scientist.

He swept his arm through the masses and pulled her to him. "We need to talk." Good Lord, even laced with anger, the deep tenor of his sensuous voice seeped into her skin and filled her with longing. With effort, she fought down the urge to squirm.

Shielding her from the rain with his umbrella, he leaned forward, caging her between him and the protesters. He stood so close she could absorb the heat radiating from his flesh. His scent assailed her senses. She blinked a fat raindrop from her lashes and tipped her head to meet his eyes. A rush of sexual energy hit her as she allowed herself a moment to admire his roguish good looks. It baffled her that a guy this hot spent his nights alone. Especially seeing the way women reacted to him.

Maybe he was gay.

She pursed her lips. "Is there going to be yelling involved?"

A muscle in his jaw clenched as his frown deepened. "It's a high probability," he assured her.

She shrugged, her damp hair falling over her shoulders. "Okay, just checking."

Sam reached out and shackled her wrist. The warmth of his skin chased the chill from her body. She kept pace as he negotiated them through the crowd and into the front lobby of his building. God, if he had this much passion when he was angry, she could only imagine how much he'd have when he was aroused. Damned if she didn't want to find out.

Once inside, he twisted around and leveled her with a glare. He muffled curses under his breath. "Do you have any idea—"

He stopped mid-sentence and hesitated. His simmering blue eyes flitted across her face before panning downward, registering every detail of her rain-soaked clothes. Had his gaze just lingered around the vicinity of her breasts?

So maybe he wasn't gay.

She acknowledged the flare of desire deep between her thighs as her body hummed in anticipation. She wondered if he could see the telltale hardening of her nipples beneath her wet, breast-hugging sweater.

She shivered, water dripping from her clothes and pooling at her feet. His features softened as his attention drifted back to her face. "We need to get you out of those clothes." Like a blanket of warmth, his seductive cadence heated her from the inside out. He brushed a damp lock from her cheek and tucked it behind her ear, an intimate gesture that shifted her hormones into overdrive. A muscle in his jaw clenched. "Right now," he insisted, his voice sounding tight as he panned her body-molding clothes a second time.

A slow, lazy grin tugged at her mouth as her lust-drunk mind envisioned those strong hands disrobing her. Her gaze journeyed over his fine, athletic body, taking in his low-slung scrubs and matching short-sleeved, loose-fitting pale green top. She devoured every delicious detail as a curious tingle rushed through her bloodstream.

His brows knit together with concern. She recognized that look. It was the same motherly look of concern she'd seen her sister-in-law Sarah give her three-year-old nephew, Matt, when he'd come down with the flu a few months back.

"Before you catch pneumonia," he added.

The grin slipped from her face as her bliss disappeared. She resisted the urge to roll her eyes heavenward. *Gay.* Throwing her hands up, she nodded in understanding. "Of course, pneumonia. We wouldn't want that, now would we?"

He slipped his arm under hers and guided her to the security counter. "I keep an extra pair of scrubs in my lab. You can wear those, and then we need to talk."

Talk!

Didn't he know talking was overrated?

Especially when there were so many other things they could be doing.

As they moved through the foyer, across the wide expanse of marble floor, Sam angled his head and took in the wet erotic vision before him.

Cat Nichols.

He was convinced the drenched she-devil had been put on earth to try his patience. Had she never heard of a damn umbrella?

His blood ignited to near boiling as he allowed himself a brief, luxurious moment to conjure up the image of him peeling off her soaked, thigh-hugging jeans and breast-molding sweater.

Fuck. His damn future was at stake, and all he could think about was sex. Terrific. That's what he got for burying himself in his work and going without the finer things in life for the last six months. And by finer, he meant Cat Nichols.

He commanded himself to redirect his thoughts as they approached the security counter. After he hastily signed her in and fitted her with a visitor's pass, he watched the sway of her lush ass as she stepped onto the waiting elevator. He closed his eyes against the flood of heat gravitating south. Lord, what he'd do to cradle that hot little backside in his palms. Temptation as he'd never before experienced swamped him, prompting his dick into action.

He clenched his jaw and bit back a moan. The last thing

he needed was a fucking hard-on in his unforgiving scrubs. A public display of his current aroused state ranked right up there with the time he'd gotten an erection during his seventh grade gym class when Jessica Johnson had worn her short shorts. It was not one of his finer moments. It had been a long time since a woman had made him feel like a lusty, hormone-driven teen on date night. And here he'd thought he'd gotten control over those unexpected risings. Talk about the second coming!

A low growl rumbled from the depths of his throat and reverberated off the metal walls, despite his best efforts to stifle it.

Cat swatted her hair from her forehead and turned around to face him. "What was that?"

Ignoring her question, he jabbed the elevator button and leaned against the wall. He met her glance but wished he hadn't. Seductive green eyes dusted with tiny flecks of honey stared up at him. *Cat eyes.* Hence the nickname, no doubt. Her blond hair hung over slender shoulders, nestling against the gentle slope of her breasts. He'd just bet that sun-kissed color hadn't come from a bottle. His fingers clenched and unclenched as his gaze dropped to her waistband. Lust clawed to the surface as he perused her. She seemed completely unaware of her allure or how much she stirred his libido and fired his blood.

"Sam?"

The sweet, melodic sound of her voice resonated through his body and pulled him back. He tried to hold on to his anger, but it melted around the edges as his eyes met hers.

"Yeah?"

"What was that you said?"

"Nothing."

Shivering, she hugged herself and leaned toward him. Cat lifted one perfect brow. "I could have sworn you just said something."

He rolled one shoulder and hedged. "The elevator is old. It makes noises," he said, shifting his stance to hide his inflated body part.

Her arousing scent reached him. A delicious combination of sweet summer rain and succulent, vine-ripened oranges. Of all things good and holy, that had to be the most seductive aroma he'd ever inhaled.

Shit, his goddamn cock just grew another inch.

Cat rubbed her palms up and down her arms. The gentleman in him urged him to offer his warmth. The man in him urged him to offer something a little farther south.

"Come here, you're freezing." Stepping into her personal space, he cradled her under his arms, warming her body with his. The snug contact created an instant air of intimacy. He felt a curious shift in his gut as she nuzzled against him and absorbed his heat.

The last few months had been hell. Total and utter hell. He'd barely been able to concentrate on his work knowing the sexy vixen lived mere minutes away in the condo across the courtyard. He wasn't sure whether it was a blessing or a curse that the positioning of their buildings provided him with a direct view of her bedroom when he stood inside his own.

He'd wanted to ask her out. In fact, he'd planned on it right after he completed his project and perfected his serum. Which would have been soon had she not written the damn article and drawn so much negative attention to him.

For the past six months his crazy schedule and deadline had left little room for extracurricular pleasures. He wasn't about to call on her until he could give her the attention she deserved, because judging by the number of men coming and going from her condo, Sam knew Cat Nichols demanded a lot of attention. And damn it, he wanted to be the guy to give it to her, not one of the six men who paraded in and out of her place at all hours while he was swamped with work.

Not that he watched and counted.

Not at all.

Not much anyway.

The truth was, Cat was exactly the kind of woman he dated. One who appeared to enjoy playing the field, and didn't seem anxious to settle down, or ask more from him than he could give.

The last thing he needed in his life was to get involved with a girl looking for a serious relationship, which made him wonder why he found the idea of Cat consorting with so many other men unsettling.

He berated himself for feeling so possessive toward her. His six-month boner and oxygen-starved brain had to be the reason he was feeling all peculiar inside. Christ, he really needed to get this girl out of his system. Surely once he appeased his body's primal urges, his thought processes would return to normal.

But he couldn't do that until he completed his project. Now, thanks to Cat's article, and the media's erroneous take on it, things at the lab were totally fucked up. Animal rights activists were pounding down his door, assuming the experimental serum would be tested on his pet chimpanzee, Rio. Due to the unexpected turn of events, the research center's board of directors had halted his experiment, which prohibited him from completing his assignment. Even the press conference his director, Reginald Smith, held hadn't assuaged protesters. Another round of curses lodged in his throat as he considered his dilemma.

He had to figure out a new game plan. Fast. But what? If only he could test the female libido enhancer on himself. Preliminary results had been a success with no side effects. He just had to run one more analysis before he could verify his findings to the grant governing board. If he failed to make his deadline, his grant money would be allotted elsewhere. He couldn't let that happen. Too many people were counting on him.

He pulled Cat tighter in his arms as the perfect solution flashed through his mind like a lightning storm. Undoubtedly, the sexy wildcat who had messed things up would never agree to such a sinfully wicked plan.

Or would she?

His body buzzed as he entertained the idea. It was the

perfect solution to his problem, really. He could complete his assignment and get the little spitfire out of his system.

The old elevator squealed, then jerked to a halt. As soon as the metal doors cleared, he linked his fingers through hers, stepped out, and ushered her down the hall. He swiped his identification card through the electronic lock and pushed the lab door open.

"After you."

Cat offered a smile and walked past him, her sweet scent lingering behind, teasing and tormenting his libido. He banked his desires, but his traitorous cock refused to obey.

Sam watched Cat catalog her surroundings before making her way over to Rio. Without taking his eyes off her, Sam moved to his desk and pulled a pair of scrubs from his drawer. His lab wasn't huge, but it was big enough for his workstation, his desk, and Rio's cage.

Hunkering down, Cat reached into the cage. Her hair spilled forward, brushing over her breasts. "Hey Rio, how are you, girl?" she asked. Gripping the bars, Rio rocked back and forth and made a hand gesture. Cat turned to face him. "What's she saying, Sam?"

"She's saying she loves you." Which Sam thought was rather odd. Rio had proved to be the jealous type. She hated when Sam brought women into the lab, or into his condo. Perhaps Rio felt a certain closeness with Cat from seeing her around the condo complex. Kind of the same way he did.

Oh boy!

It occurred to him that he was far more intrigued by Cat

than he would have liked. She unearthed things in him he preferred to keep buried. Sam had had his fair share of physical relations with women, but had avoided making deep connections. After his mother bailed, leaving a family behind, his father had a plethora of female companions. They'd hang around for a while, long enough for Sam to form a bond, then, just like his mother, when something *bigger and better* came along, they would up and leave without warning.

Sam did a mental reminder of his rules. Never get too interested and never let them get too close, because in the end, all women he got emotionally attached to ended up walking out.

One perfect brow arched. "You taught her sign language?" Cat climbed to her feet.

Sam shrugged. "Yeah." He pointed to the small bathroom. "You can get changed in there. I'll make coffee."

CATHRYN FOX

A multi-published author in the romance genre, Cathryn has two teenagers who keep her busy and a husband who is convinced he can turn her into a mixed martial arts fan. Cathryn can never find balance in her life and is always trying to keep up with emails, Facebook, Pinterest, and Twitter. She spends her days writing page-turning books filled with heat and heart, and loves to hear from her readers.